D1473447

DATE DUE

DISCARD

This item is Due on
or before Date shown.

ON AN AMERICAN DAY

VOLUME 1

Story Voyages Through History
1750–1899

Rona Arato
Illustrated by Ben Shannon

Owl kids

Owlkids Books Inc.
10 Lower Spadina Avenue, Suite 400, Toronto, Ontario M5V 2Z2
www.owlkids.com

Library and Archives Canada Cataloguing in Publication

Arato, Rona
        On an American day : story voyages through history, 1750-1899 / Rona
Arato ; illustrated by Ben Shannon.

Issued also in electronic format.
ISBN 978-1-926818-91-7 (v. 1, bound).--ISBN 978-1-926818-92-4 (v. 1, pbk.)

        I. Shannon, Ben II. Title.

PS8601.R35O58 2011   jC813'.6   C2011-900243-4

Library of Congress Control Number: 2010943327

E-book ISBN: 978-1-926818-93-1

Design: Samantha Edwards

 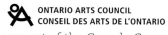

We acknowledge the financial support of the Canada Council for the Arts,
the Ontario Arts Council, the Government of Canada through the Canada
Book Fund (CBF), and the Government of Ontario through the Ontario Media
Development Corporation's Book Initiative for our publishing activities.

Manufactured by WKT Co. Ltd.
Manufactured in Shenzhen, Guangdong, China in March 2011
Job #10CB3834

A   B   C   D   E   F

Publisher of Chirp, chickaDEE and OWL
www.owlkids.com

ON AN AMERICAN DAY

VOLUME 1

★ ★ ★ ★ ★ **Contents**

A BOY WITH A DRUM

A DIFFERENT KIND OF FRIEND

A RECIPE FOR VICTORY

A NEW WAY TO SEE

A GOLD NUGGET FOR ADAM

NO MORE MASTERS

THE LAST RAIL

FINDING SARAH

A NEW HOPE

As always, for Paul
—Rona

Dear Reader,

American history is full of courage and conflict, hope and catastrophe, adventures, missteps, and above all, new beginnings. This book covers the years 1750 to 1899—a period during which a once-small colonial outpost fought and won a war for independence from Great Britain, endured its own civil war, and eventually became a nation that stretched from the Atlantic to the Pacific.

When European explorers first arrived, they found a rich land filled with forests, wildlife, and bodies of fresh water—as well as a large population of Native peoples. Early settlers followed, seeking a refuge from religious persecution back in Europe. Leaders developed a democratic system of government guaranteeing freedom of religion, speech, and thought that was unique for its time.

This system, however, did not apply to everyone. As the population spread, Natives lost their land and saw their way of life destroyed. Slavery flourished in the southern states. It took a civil war to free the slaves and then another hundred years for the civil rights movement to enforce many of their hard-won freedoms. In spite of these problems, America shone as a beacon of democracy that attracted immigrants from around the world.

That same period saw the growth of great cities such as Philadelphia and Chicago; the start of the Industrial Revolution; the beginning of mass communication; the launch of a transcontinental railroad; and the start of social services such as the American Red Cross and urban settlement houses to help the poor. All of these developments helped the young nation grow into a strong, influential country.

As you read their stories, ask yourself what you have in common with the children you meet in this book. How are you the same? How are you different? What can you learn from their stories, and what, if you could talk to them, would they learn from you?

After reading the book, ask your family to tell you their stories and write them down. You can keep them in a journal or turn them into stories of your own. Someday you can share them with your children. Or maybe, you too will write a book. Learning about people and places in other times is exciting. So turn the page to meet nine boys and girls who are just like you in some ways, and in others, not like you at all.

Rona Arato

A DIFFERENT KIND OF FRIEND

Philadelphia, Pennsylvania, 1765

MORNING... Patrick stared into his bowl of porridge.

"Patrick, finish your breakfast."

His head snapped up as his mother's voice cut through his thoughts. "I am almost finished, Ma."

"It looks to me like you are playing instead of eating. You should be ashamed of yourself, wasting good, solid food. Why in Ireland…"

"In Ireland we were farmers and ate potatoes." Patrick's father, Sean O'Brien strode into the room. A tall man, he had to stoop to avoid hitting his head on the doorframe. "And do you know why?"

"Because potatoes were all that the British landowners would let Catholic farmers keep of our crops," Patrick recited.

"And what else?" asked his father.

"Here, thanks to William Penn, we are free to be whatever we want and to eat whatever we want."

"Good boy. William Penn established Pennsylvania." Mr. O'Brien nodded his approval. "Never forget why we came to this land, Patrick. So wipe that sour look from your face. Look at your sister. She's as bright as a sunny day."

Meagan gave her father a gap-toothed smile.

"She does not have to spend all day in the market next to Protestant boys."

"And what is wrong with working beside them?"

"I am not comfortable."

"Patrick!" His father gave him a stern look. "That is the kind of thinking we left Ireland to escape. Those boys mean you no harm."

"In Ireland, they were our enemies."

"And here we all live together peacefully."

"Can I come to the market with you?" Meagan gave her father a wistful look.

"When you are older. Now you must stay home with your mother to learn how to sew and cook."

"I cannot cook," said Patrick.

"You can carve wooden things, like Father does," said Meagan. She pointed to a pair of maple wood candlesticks in the middle of the table.

"That is because one day I want to be a furniture maker like father," said Patrick.

"And you, Meagan, will sew beautiful clothes for the whole family." Mr. O'Brien pointed to the spinning wheel in the corner of the room. "Is your mother not teaching you to spin wool?"

"Meagan and I dye the wool and then sew it into capes and pants and dresses," said Mrs. O'Brien.

"I still want to go to the market," said Meagan, only slightly satisfied by this answer. She looked around the one room that was their home, with its brick fireplace, the maple wood furniture their father had made, and her mother's lacy curtains fluttering at the windows. She sighed and reached for her rag doll, Polly. "You are a girl too, Polly, so you will stay home with me."

Mr. O'Brien turned to Patrick. "We had better go now. We still have to load the wagon. And I want to be at the market early so we are ready for the day's business when it comes."

I must remember that we are no longer in Ireland, and I must not resent Protestants, as I did there, for keeping us poor.

Mr. O'Brien flicked the reins and the family's horse moved forward. Patrick sat on the wooden seat beside his father. Behind him were his father's hand-carved bowls, boxes of wooden spoons and candlesticks, chairs, a table, and a solid oak dresser, along with several bolts of his mother's wool.

The June morning was warm. The air smelled of new leaves and fruit blossoms. After the dampness of Ireland, the Philadelphia sun was welcome. As they moved through Philadelphia's streets, Patrick studied the people they passed. The men wore pants that came to just below their knees, with woolen stockings. Their shirts were loose, like the shirt he wore, with ruffles around the neck and cuffs. Most men wore wigs. They were made of human hair, goat hair, or horse hair. The poorest men wore wigs made of thread. The women wore long dresses dyed bright yellow, purple, red, or blue and covered their hair with lacy caps. *I do like it here,* Patrick thought as they drove through the town. *I must remember that we are no longer in Ireland, and I must not resent Protestants, as I did there, for keeping us poor.*

As they rode, Patrick marveled, as he always did, at the splendor of his adopted city. "Look, Pa. That is Mr. Franklin."

Benjamin Franklin was a well-known figure in Philadelphia. He was a statesman, an inventor, and a publisher. Mr. Franklin wore a red waistcoat, a white ruffled shirt, and dark pants. His shoes were polished and had shiny gold buckles. Unlike most men, he did not wear a wig, and his light brown hair ringed the top of his head, which was bald, and fell almost to his shoulders. As Patrick watched, Mr. Franklin mounted the steps of the public library he had founded. He believed that since most people could not afford to buy books, there should be a place where they might read them for free.

"Pa, Mr. Franklin is a great man, is he not?"

"A very great man. He believes, as did William Penn, that all people are equal and deserve to live in freedom. We are lucky to live in such a place." He turned his head and looked into Patrick's eyes. "Never forget that, Son."

"Yes, Pa." Patrick swallowed. It wasn't often that Pa was this serious. *It was what I said about Protestants that has made him talk like this. He thinks like Mr. Penn. He wants me to think that way, too.*

"Here we are." Mr. O'Brien turned into the marketplace with its open-air stalls selling meat, cheese, vegetables, clothing, and tools. In spite of the early hour, there was a bustle of activity as farmers and merchants set out their wares. He pulled back on the reins and their horse clip-clopped to a halt in front of the family's stall. Many of the stalls were run by Quaker families who came into town on market days. They wore neat, plain clothing. One such farmer and his wife were setting out their cheeses and eggs and baskets of potatoes, onions, and carrots in the booth next to the O'Briens' stall. They nodded "good day," as Patrick and his father jumped down and began unloading their wares. On the other side, Mr. Cohen, a chandler, was unpacking his

candles. In Ireland, the O'Briens had made their own candles—a laborious and time-consuming task. Here, they could afford to buy Mr. Cohen's graceful tapers made of animal fat with sturdy cotton wicks.

Patrick worked quickly. First he set out the smaller items—candlesticks, bowls, and wooden spoons. Then he and his father unloaded four maple wood chairs and a table. Patrick helped his father lift the table and set it beside the stall.

"Ah, such beautiful craftsmanship." Mr. Cohen walked over and ran his hand along the tabletop. "You are very talented."

"As are you." Mr. O'Brien smiled. "Your candles add warmth *and* beauty to our home."

Patrick glanced at Mr. Cohen, who beamed with pleasure. Beside him, his son, Jacob, shuffled his feet. A shy boy, Jacob was more comfortable with books than with candles, but he faithfully came to market each week to help his father. Patrick knew that the Cohens were Jewish. In Ireland he hadn't known any Jews, although the priests had said that those who did not believe in the Lord Jesus Christ should be feared. *Jacob doesn't look like someone I should be afraid of,* Patrick thought. In Ireland, all their neighbors, family, and friends had been Catholic. They kept to themselves and avoided the British and the Protestants. Here he was expected to get along with everyone. It was all quite confusing.

By now the market was busy. Patrick watched his father deal with customers. *Sean O'Brien has the gift of blarney,* his grandmother used to say. And indeed, his father was comfortable talking to everyone. Each time he sold an item

Patrick took the money, gave change, and placed the coins in a metal box. His father's work was beautiful, and many people stopped by to admire it. By noon, the table and chairs had been sold and only a few bowls remained.

"A good morning's work." Mr. O'Brien surveyed the nearly empty stall. "We have earned a rest." He opened the box and took out two coins. "Buy us fresh buns from the baker's stall. They will go well with the cheese and apples your mother packed for our lunch."

Jacob doesn't look like someone I should be afraid of, Patrick thought.

Patrick walked to the bake stall. The smell was irresistible.

"Good day, ma'am," he said to the Quaker woman, who was handing a loaf of crusty bread to a woman in a bright yellow dress.

She turned to Patrick. "And what can I do for thee, my good young man?"

Patrick asked for two buns and was fishing the money from his pocket when a commotion caught his attention. He turned to see a dark-haired boy about his age struggling with two older boys. One was tall with ham-sized fists. The other was built square, like a brick. Both were shouting names at the younger boy, whom Patrick recognized as Jacob Cohen. The tall boy shoved Jacob. His friend yanked off the younger boy's hat, threw it on the ground, and stomped on it. When Jacob went down to retrieve it, his attacker smacked him on the side of his head.

Without thinking, Patrick raced over and pushed the attacker. His friend grabbed Patrick from behind and knocked him to the ground. Patrick struggled to his feet. He was short but wiry, and he used this to his advantage. Dancing around the bigger boys' legs, he dodged their blows and landed his own. Whap! A meaty fist smashed into his mouth. Patrick tasted blood.

He bent over and used his head as a battering ram to charge into the brick-shaped boy's middle, sending him crashing into a fruit stall. A mound of apples tumbled off the wooden table and rolled into the gutter. The tall boy grabbed Patrick by the collar, lifting him into the air and swinging him around like a ribbon on a maypole. Hair flopped into Patrick's eyes, blood dripped from his split lip, and his stomach heaved. He blinked and saw Jacob bent over double. Head down, Patrick smashed into the tall boy's knees. As they buckled, Patrick was dropped with a dusty thud. Jacob shot Patrick a triumphant grin—Patrick tried to smile back, but his split lip made it too painful. Instead he waved his fist as he struggled to his feet.

By this time a crowd had gathered. Patrick heard his father's voice boom over the din. "Up! Get up, all of you! And what do you ruffians think you are doing, fighting like a pack of hungry dogs over a bone? Have I not taught you better than this, Patrick?"

"I..., I..." Patrick gestured toward Jacob, who was using his sleeve to mop the blood pouring from his nose. Patrick noticed that his left eye was swollen shut. He looked at the two boys who had started the fight. One had a cut on his ear; the other was clutching his stomach, as if to keep its contents from spilling out.

Mr. O'Brien handed Jacob a handkerchief and then turned to Patrick. "I'm waiting for an explanation."

"They started it," Patrick said. He turned to point out his attackers, but they had disappeared into the market crowd.

"Excuse me, sir," said Jacob. "They were beating on *me* and *he* came to my rescue." He pointed at Patrick.

"And why were they doing that, lad?"

The boy looked down at his feet. "Because I am a Jew," he said in a voice so low that they could barely hear him.

"Speak up," Mr. O'Brien ordered.

"I am Jewish."

"I see." Mr. O'Brien put a finger under his chin and examined his face. "And what is your name, son?"

"Jacob. Jacob Cohen."

"Ah, now I recognize you. You are the chandler's son. Jacob, I think you had best come home with us. Mrs. O'Brien will clean you up before you scare your parents to death. I will tell your father that I asked you to help us carry the table and chairs because they are so heavy."

AFTERNOON... "Oh my!" Patrick's mother shook her head as the boys straggled into the house. "What on Earth has happened?"

"It seems our boy here was defending his friend from a gang of bullies."

"He's not my..." Patrick started and then caught himself. *Was Jacob his new friend? Did sharing a fight in the streets make them friends?*

Jacob turned to Patrick. "Why did you help me?"

Patrick looked at him. Why indeed?

"I hate bullies," Patrick blurted out. "I was beaten up in Ireland by Protestants for being Catholic."

"Now, boys, enough talk of beatings and bullies," said Mrs. O'Brien. "Go wash up and then come in for something to eat."

The boys went outside to the water pump. "Ooh, that feels good," Jacob said as he splashed cold water onto his face. He took the handle and pumped water for Patrick.

"You look like you were kicked by a horse." Jacob pointed to Patrick's face.

"You should see yourself," said Patrick. They laughed.

Back in the house they joined the O'Briens at the table. Suddenly Jacob looked nervous. "I should go home."

"First eat something," said Mrs. O'Brien. She handed him a plate with a thick slice of bread slathered with butter. "You need energy after your...experience."

Still Jacob hesitated. "I, I thank you, ma'am, but I cannot..." He broke off.

"Cannot what?" asked Patrick.

"I cannot eat in your house." Jacob lowered his eyes. He looked miserable.

Patrick glared at him. "You mean our food is not good enough for you?"

"Yes, of course your food is good. It is only that..." He stopped, bit his lip, and then spoke. "I can only eat kosher food."

"What is kosher food?" Patrick scoffed.

"Patrick." His father gave him a warning look. "Please respect Jacob's traditions as you would have him respect ours."

Patrick shrugged. If Jacob wanted to be rude, that was his business. Patrick took a big bite of his bread and chewed enthusiastically, to show Jacob what he was missing.

EVENING... After the supper dishes were cleared and washed, Mrs. O'Brien lit candles and the family gathered in front of the fireplace. She sat in the rocking chair and took out the quilt she was making. Patrick noted that his mother was always working on a quilt, either for the family or as a gift for a neighbor or a donation for the poor. Patrick picked up a piece of wood he was carving into a cradle for Meagan's doll, Polly. It was going to be her birthday gift. His father settled down to read from the *Pennsylvania Gazette*, the newspaper that Mr. Franklin published. Meagan sat on a blanket on the floor playing with Polly. The house was quiet. The only sounds were the crackle of wood in the fireplace and the rustle of Mr. O'Brien's newspaper. A rap on the door broke the silence.

> *"Unfortunately, there are bullies everywhere. They were in England, where we come from, and they are even here, in Mr. Penn's free colony."*

"Who can that be?" Mrs. O'Brien looked up from her sewing.

Mr. O'Brien stood, walked to the door, and opened it. "Mr. Cohen and Jacob, please come in."

"Thank you."

Mr. Cohen stepped uncertainly into the room. He was a taller, older version of Jacob, with dark hair flecked with gray, brown eyes, and a serious expression.

"Please, won't you sit down?" Mrs. O'Brien waved them to chairs by the table.

"No, no, thank you. We will only stay for a minute," said Mr. Cohen. "We have come to thank you for helping Jacob this afternoon." Mr. Cohen looked at Patrick. He pushed his glasses up his nose. Patrick noted they were bifocals, another of Mr. Franklin's inventions. "You were very brave, young man. What prompted you to do it?"

Patrick returned his look. "I hate bullies."

Mr. Cohen smiled. "Unfortunately, there are bullies everywhere. They were in England, where we come from, and they are even here, in Mr. Penn's free colony."

"In Ireland, the Protestants hate the Catholics," said Patrick.

"I do not hate you," said Jacob.

"You are not Protestant."

"Do not blame all Protestants for the bad deeds of a few." Mr. Cohen tugged at his beard. "Mr. Penn and his Quakers are Protestant. Mr. Franklin is a Protestant, as are many other kind and fair people."

Patrick's mother stepped forward. "Please, let us all sit at the table. Mr. Cohen, I understand that you do not eat our food, but will you accept a cup of tea?"

"It will be my pleasure. Please, Mrs. O'Brien, do not take it as a criticism of your cooking. It is just that as Jews, we eat only kosher food."

"Mr. Cohen, what is kosher food?" asked Meagan when they were seated.

Mr. Cohen rested his chin on his hands. When he answered, his voice was thoughtful. "We eat food that conforms to Jewish law as set out in the Bible. We do not mix meat and dairy. We only eat animals that chew their cud, like cows. That means we cannot eat the meat of animals such as pigs, rabbits, or hares. And we do not eat shellfish such as oysters or clams."

"But why wouldn't Jacob eat bread and butter?" asked Patrick.

Mr. Cohen turned to Patrick's mother.

"Mrs. O'Brien, do you bake with lard?"

"Of course." She nodded.

"And lard is fat from a pig," said Patrick. "I suppose it is like Catholics not eating meat on Fridays."

"Every religion has traditions," said Mr. O'Brien. "And here, we respect all of them."

As the Cohens prepared to leave, Jacob took Patrick aside. "I think we will be friends now."

"I guess fighting off bullies makes us friends," Patrick agreed. "In Ireland, my best friend and I had a secret sign. It was our special way of communicating. I think you and I should do the same. That way we can talk so the bullies will not understand us."

"I like that idea," said Jacob. "I will think about it tonight."

"Tomorrow," said Patrick, "let us meet and decide what our sign will be."

The candles had burnt low. It was time for bed. Patrick went outside to use the privy, a wooden structure that served as a toilet. Once he was back inside, he climbed up to the attic, changed into his nightdress, and knelt beside the straw mattress that was his bed. It was time for his nightly prayers. As he said the familiar words, he thought of Jacob. Did he too pray at night? What other traditions, besides eating kosher food, did he keep? And more important, what games did he like to play? Could he fly a kite? Shoot marbles or push a hoop? There were so many things to learn about his new friend.

Patrick climbed into bed and pulled the quilt up to his chin. Beside him, Meagan lay on her mattress talking to Polly. Patrick smiled a half smile—as far as his wounded lip would allow. Girls made such a fuss over their dolls. Not like boys, who had important things to do like coming up with secret codes. *Maybe Jacob and I could even come up with our own secret language,* he thought. *With our own language, no one will dare bully us.* And that, he thought, would be the best thing of all. ✪

A DIFFERENT KIND OF FRIEND

Religious Freedom in Philadelphia

William Penn treated the Lenape Natives who lived on the land he was granted with great respect. He learned their language and visited them often.

In 1681, King Charles II of England granted what is now Pennsylvania to William Penn in payment for a debt the king owed Penn's father, Admiral William Penn. Penn called the colony Sylvania, which means "woods." The king changed the name to Pennsylvania. Even though Penn was granted the land by the king, he would not settle any part of it without first buying the claims of the Native peoples who lived there.

The town of Philadelphia was established in 1682, and the Charter of Privileges, which set up an elected legislature and guaranteed freedom of religion, was adopted later that year. By the time of the American Revolution, Philadelphia was the biggest city in the Colonies and the second largest English-speaking city in the world, after London, England.

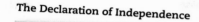

The Declaration of Independence

Philadelphia, Pennsylvania

Benjamin Franklin

Benjamin Franklin

Philadelphia's liberal environment encouraged many firsts in America, including the first public school, the first treatise against slavery, the first public library, the first volunteer fire department, and the first hospital. Many of these innovations were the work of Benjamin Franklin.

Benjamin Franklin was a publisher, scientist, inventor, statesman, and philosopher. Among his many inventions were the lightning rod, bifocal glasses, and the Franklin stove, which allowed people to warm their homes more safely than using a fireplace. Franklin is best known for his part in the American Revolution. Franklin was elected to the Second Continental Congress, where he helped draft the Declaration of Independence and was one of its signers. He was instrumental in getting the French to support the Colonists against England. After the war he served as a delegate to the Constitutional Convention and signed the Constitution.

A PLACE IN HISTORY

A LEGACY OF TOLERANCE

Philadelphia was founded by Quakers. They are a religious group that believes in equality and tolerance. The city is famously nicknamed the City of Brotherly Love. Philadelphia became a center of the abolitionist movement leading up to the Civil War. It played an important part in the Underground Railroad. Escaping slaves found refuge in the "safe houses" of Pennsylvania. Because slave hunters were constantly chasing runaway slaves, many of the refugee slaves followed the Underground Railroad all the way to Canada. Camp William Penn in Cheltenham, Pennsylvania, was the first federal training camp for black soldiers. It was established in 1863, and 11,000 volunteer soldiers were trained there to fight for the Union Army. After the war many of these newly freed blacks settled in and around Philadelphia.

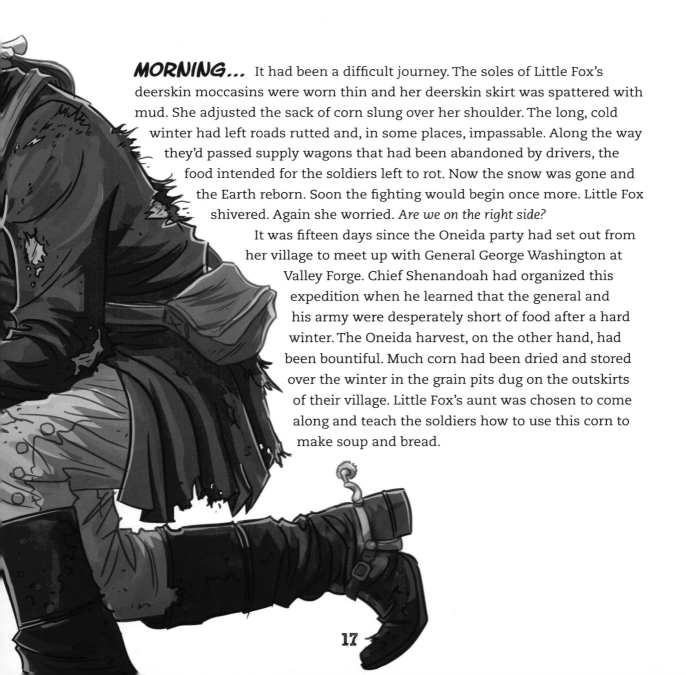

A RECIPE FOR VICTORY

Valley Forge, Pennsylvania, 1778

MORNING... It had been a difficult journey. The soles of Little Fox's deerskin moccasins were worn thin and her deerskin skirt was spattered with mud. She adjusted the sack of corn slung over her shoulder. The long, cold winter had left roads rutted and, in some places, impassable. Along the way they'd passed supply wagons that had been abandoned by drivers, the food intended for the soldiers left to rot. Now the snow was gone and the Earth reborn. Soon the fighting would begin once more. Little Fox shivered. Again she worried. *Are we on the right side?*

It was fifteen days since the Oneida party had set out from her village to meet up with General George Washington at Valley Forge. Chief Shenandoah had organized this expedition when he learned that the general and his army were desperately short of food after a hard winter. The Oneida harvest, on the other hand, had been bountiful. Much corn had been dried and stored over the winter in the grain pits dug on the outskirts of their village. Little Fox's aunt was chosen to come along and teach the soldiers how to use this corn to make soup and bread.

Her aunt was a wise woman indeed and knew the colonists very well. Unlike Little Fox and most other Oneida, she spoke their language and was even given an English name by them: Polly Cooper. When she had asked her niece to join her, Little Fox was honored to be part of this expedition—but she still had her doubts.

"Is that really the camp just over that ridge?" asked Little Fox, exhausted.

"Yes, finally." Polly sighed and stopped, putting her sack of corn on the ground. She sensed Little Fox's uneasiness. "And do you still have doubts about our mission?"

"My brother Lone Wolf thinks that General Washington is not right to fight the British," said Little Fox. "The rest of the Iroquois nation agrees with him. Why are we not siding with our own people?"

"Chief Shenandoah believes that the future lies with the colonists and we should side with them," said Brown Fox, one of the sixty warriors who had come to carry the several hundred bushels of corn and protect Polly and Little Fox. "He believes the British will be defeated."

"What if the British win?" asked Little Fox. "Then we will be on the wrong side."

"My son speaks wisely," said a warrior standing beside Brown Fox. "The colonists will win this battle because they are fighting for their freedom." He held up a hand toughened by many seasons of hard work. "The Oneida believe in their cause."

"Gray Owl is right," said Polly.

"But what will happen to us if the British *do* win?" Little Fox pleaded again.

"We will face that situation if it happens," said Gray Owl calmly.

"I have heard that General Washington is a great warrior who will lead his people to victory," said Polly, trying to comfort Little Fox. "Our corn will help them survive." She picked up her satchel and began walking. The others followed.

Little Fox respected the wisdom of Polly and Gray Owl. But she also respected her brother Lone Wolf. He believed in the British. *I wish Lone Wolf were with us,* she thought. *He would be a comfort to me. Or at least someone closer to my age to be with.*

"We have arrived," shouted Gray Owl back to the rear of their group. The men cheered with relief.

The party passed the sentries and entered the Continental Army camp. Little Fox saw a vast open field with soldiers everywhere. Wood cabins were scattered across the ground, amid a forest of tree stumps. *I know where they got the wood for their dwellings,* thought Little Fox. She wrinkled her nose.

"I smell it, too," Polly nodded. She turned to an officer who had come to greet them. "What is that awful smell?"

"That, ma'am, is the smell of five months of unwashed bodies and poor sanitation," said the officer. "At night, these horrid vapors spread through the camp. They become less noxious during the day, and then at nightfall, they rise again." He looked at the bags of corn the women were carrying. "I see you have brought us food. That will help restore health and morale. Maybe you can help us do something about the smell later, too." He gave her a weary smile.

> *"I have heard that General Washington is a great warrior who will lead his people to victory."*

Little Fox strained to understand him.

"We have two hundred and fifty bushels of corn," said Polly. "We have already scraped the kernels from the cobs, so they are ready to cook. We will teach your men to make corn soup and cornbread."

"We are grateful for your help." The officer saluted and walked off.

Now that they were in the camp, Little Fox saw just how bad the soldiers' condition was. Their uniforms were frayed and their shoes had holes; indeed some men did not have shoes at all. Yet an air of hope pervaded the camp.

"Spring is a powerful tonic," Polly said, as if reading Little Fox's mind. She turned as a man in a blue cape and three-cornered hat approached them.

"Thank you for coming." The man held out his hand. "I am General George Washington. I and my men are indebted to you for your kindness."

Little Fox looked at the general with interest. He was one of the tallest men she had ever seen. His light brown hair was dusted with white powder and pulled back with a dark ribbon. She had heard talk of this commander who was leading the Continental Army. His people loved him, and she could see why. He had a kindly face and seemed genuinely concerned with the fate of his men.

"Please let me know if I can help you in any way." The general smiled.

As they walked to the storehouse, Little Fox studied the camp. Polly had explained that the general chose this site because it was removed from the British army. Valley Forge was on a river bend, surrounded by water on three sides. That made it easy to defend. Maybe so, but over the winter,

living conditions had deteriorated. There weren't enough blankets or medical supplies. The log cabins were cold and drafty. Many of the men were sick.

Conversations in English—none of which Little Fox could understand or join—bombarded her ears and added to her confusion. *What if Polly and I or other Oneida become sick? Can such a worn-out army really defeat the British? Is it possible that they…*

"Little Fox!" Polly stood looking down at her. "Stop dreaming! We must get to work."

AFTERNOON… The arrival of the Oneida was greeted with enthusiasm by the soldiers milling about the camp. A number of women—mothers, wives, and sisters—were also there, tending the sick, doing laundry, and helping where they could. Still, there was much to be done.

"Your people have come here before," said a soldier who was helping Polly and Little Fox store the bushels of corn. He scratched his head. Little Fox squirmed at the thought of the lice that were most likely nesting in his matted hair. "Where are you from?" he asked.

"We are of the Oneida nation." *The Iroquois will not help here because they are siding with the British,* thought Polly. She turned to the man who was in charge of the cooking shed. "I am Polly Cooper. What is your name?"

"Ben, ma'am. Sergeant Ben Stevens." The man reached into a sack, scooped out a handful of corn kernels, and popped them into his mouth.

"Spit that out!" Polly said. "Do not swallow."

Startled, the soldier bent over and spit out the corn.

"I thought you brought it for us to eat," he sputtered.

"After it is cooked!" Polly sighed. "Our corn is very hard. It must be cooked for many hours before you can eat it. Otherwise, it will expand in your stomach and could kill you. To boil it, I will need a large kettle, water, and a good strong fire."

"Yes, ma'am." Sgt. Stevens moved closer to Little Fox. She recoiled from his foul breath. Were all the soldiers in such bad shape? At this point, she saw that the Oneida men were poking around the camp, talking to the troops and taking interest in everything they saw—especially in the soldiers' weapons.

"Should they be doing that?" she asked Polly.

"General Washington has no objection to natural curiosity," Polly responded. "He is welcoming them as if they were his own."

Little Fox's attention was caught by voices from an open field. She looked over to see what was happening.

A portly man in a long coat, a three-cornered hat, and high black boots was watching a line of soldiers load their guns. But the man spoke a language that Little Fox did not recognize. An aide beside him translated his words into English. Immediately sensing her niece's curiosity, Polly asked what was happening.

"That is Baron von Steuben," Sgt. Stevens said excitedly. "He came here from Prussia during the winter and has been training us to fight the British. Watch them load their muskets. Before he came, it took us nineteen motions to reload. He taught us how to do it in only fifteen! That means we can shoot faster at the enemy."

"What else has he taught you?" Polly

asked the sergeant.

"The proper formations to use in a battle, and how to march in step without a drum."

"How do you do that?"

"You watch the officer at the head of the column and do what he does. Soon we will see if the baron's instructions have made us better at fighting. Now that it is spring, we are ready to meet the British. We will chase those Redcoats back to England, where they belong."

As Polly explained this to Little Fox, the baron was leading a column of men marching with a cadence that showed the success of his teaching. All at once, Little Fox thought again of her brother. Lone Wolf had called Washington's soldiers a rag-tag group who would never win a war. *I wish he could watch these men march*, she thought.

"Come, Little Fox," said Polly. "Those soldiers will drill better on full stomachs."

Little Fox took one last look at the field and then walked with Polly into the cookhouse. But as she did, she spied a shadowy figure skulking among the trees at the edge of the clearing. Then Polly called and she scurried to join her.

Polly was stirring a mixture of corn kernels, water, and lye in the kettle that Sgt. Stevens had set up for them. "It is cooked. Come help me hull the corn," she called out as Little Fox approached.

Sgt. Stevens stared at the blackened kernels. "The men may be hungry, ma'am, but I doubt they will eat lye."

Polly smiled. "Sergeant, we are far from finished. This corn soup will take the rest of the day to cook. This is what we do next." She poured the corn mixture into a wood cylinder with a woven bottom. "Little Fox, pour water over the corn while I hull it." She gave Sgt. Stevens a stern look. "Pay close attention. I will have you make the next batch."

Sgt. Stevens shuffled his feet. "Yes, ma'am. But I still do not think…"

"The Oneida people have been eating this corn soup for a thousand years, and we have survived," Polly smiled kindly. She handed Little Fox a hunk of salt pork. "Little Fox here will cut this in small chunks and add it to the corn. Then we add water and cook the soup for ten hours."

"Ten hours?" Sgt. Stevens looked horrified.

"Yes, Sergeant. It will not be ready for tonight's supper, but we will eat it tomorrow."

While the soup cooked, Little Fox helped Polly grind corn into flour for cornbread. For this they used a hollowed-out tree trunk and a large stone pestle. When the corn was finely ground, they would add water and bake it in the fire. As she worked, Little Fox hummed a song under her breath. It was one her mother had taught her when she was little. It was about a small bird building a nest in a tree. So engrossed was she that she almost missed the sharp whistle coming from behind the storehouse. Something about it tweaked her memory, and she stopped her work to listen. There it was again, a whistle she had heard for most of her life. *Lone Wolf.*

She jumped to her feet. *Is it possible that*

"Now that it is spring, we are ready to meet the British. We will chase those Redcoats back to England, where they belong."

my brother is here? She looked around the camp but saw only the soldiers and Polly. Yet no one but she and Lone Wolf knew their secret whistle. Setting the pestle back into the bowl, she moved stealthily toward the storehouse and peered around it. There, huddled in its shadow, was her brother.

"Lone Wolf, what are you doing here?" She rushed to his side and gasped at the sticky red stain on his tunic. "Are you hurt?"

Lone Wolf was crouched over. She repeated her question, and he groaned and clutched his side.

"First we must get you medical care," she said. "Then you can tell me what has happened."

Fortunately, Lone Wolf's wound was not serious. Little Fox eventually got him to a cabin that was used as an infirmary, where a camp nurse cleansed and bandaged it. When they were alone, Little Fox turned to her brother. "Now tell me what happened and why you are here."

Lone Wolf leaned against the wall of the cabin. His black hair was slick with sweat; the blood drained from his mahogany skin. "A British sniper shot me as I made my way through the woods. It was not a deep wound, but it got worse quickly."

"And just how did you know I was here?"

"Before I left, I heard that the chief was planning to send a group of our people to Valley Forge, and that Polly Cooper and a young girl were among them. I hoped that girl was you." He gave his sister a weak

smile. "I got lucky. I'm not sure how much farther I would have made it."

"But what of your feelings about the colonists? I thought you believed in the British?"

"I did." Lone Wolf winced with pain. "I no longer feel that way."

Little Fox looked at him with interest. "What changed your mind?"

"You mean besides being shot?" Her brother laughed before his black eyes assumed a faraway look. "I have met many people since I left our home. I heard them talk of their love of freedom. And I began to understand what they want to create. The British laws are unfair. Yet now that I see this camp, I fear for the colonists' ability to win."

"Things *are* desperate here," Little Fox began, "but these soldiers show much spirit. They even have someone from a kingdom called Prussia who is training them. They claim to have learned much from him— they looked very impressive marching."

"I saw them, too," nodded her brother. "I *would* like to trust them."

Little Fox took his hand. "I am glad that you are here. I must go find Polly and tell her the news."

EVENING... Little Fox and her brother joined Polly and a group of Oneida men who had gathered with a few colonial soldiers around a campfire.

"Lone Wolf! Welcome!" Gray Owl motioned for him to sit, quickly showing concern. "I thought you were fighting for

"I do not know who is right, but I will help the colonists because I too believe they will win the battle for this land."

the British."

"He has decided to join our side," said Brown Fox.

"I do wish to fight with my brothers," Lone Wolf said, "as long as we are certain that these people will treat us fairly if they win."

"I trust General Washington," said Brown Fox. "He has promised that he will respect our freedom and our lands."

"Except," said Lone Wolf, getting agitated, "people say what they must to get what they want...and the general wants our help."

"Then why are *you* here?" asked Gray Owl, his calm voice relieving the tension. "If you do not wish to fight for our cause, why have you come?"

"I came to find my sister." Lone Wolf turned to Little Fox. "But I am starting to believe this is the right side to fight for. How about you, Sister? Are *you* convinced that the Colonists are right to be fighting the British?"

Little Fox hesitated. Until today, she had been undecided. But watching the fervor of these men, in spite of their wretched condition, had convinced her they truly believed in their quest. So had seeing outsiders like the baron helping them in their cause. She turned to her brother. "I think that we are smart to help the colonists because they are the future."

"Big words for such a little girl," laughed her brother, but then his expression turned serious. "I do not know who is right, but I will help the colonists because I too believe they will win the battle for this land."

At that moment, Sgt. Stevens appeared at the edge of the group. "I apologize for the interruption. I came to thank you for the food, Miss Cooper. Please tell your group on behalf of our men." He swept off his hat and bowed to the Oneida.

Polly smiled. "So then you liked the cornbread, Sergeant?"

"It was delicious."

"Then you will like our soup."

"The cornbread does not have lye in it."

"You will not taste the lye in the soup."

"I am certain that we won't," answered a deep voice. "But first, Miss Cooper, I wish to sample this bread, of which I have heard so much."

"*General Washington!*" The sergeant snapped to attention.

The general turned to Polly. "And who is our newest guest?"

"This is my nephew Lone Wolf," Polly replied. "He wants to join your army."

General Washington studied him. "And where has he been until now?"

"With the British," Polly explained, as Lone Wolf looked up into the general's eyes. "He says that he has much

information to give you."

"You are certain that he is not a spy?" the general asked Polly.

"I will vouch for him."

General Washington clapped a hand on Lone Wolf's shoulder. "Tell him we will talk tomorrow. I am eager to hear what he has to tell us. Now I must go. I have invited your chief to join me for supper."

"General Washington seems a good man," said Lone Wolf later that evening.

"If only he could clean the air." Little Fox wrinkled her nose. As dusk settled, the noxious odors that had greeted her this morning had returned. She turned to her brother. "What will you do now?"

"I understand that the Oneida are to join with up Colonel Morgan, whose corps is scouting enemy lines. I will be with them." He touched his side. "As long as my wound heals enough. And you, Little Fox? What will you do?"

"I will stay here with Polly to care for the soldiers until the war is over. Then," she said looking up at the sky, "I will go home. The home this general has promised he will honor." ✪

A RECIPE FOR VICTORY
The Winter at Valley Forge

Colonists were very unhappy with British rule. In New York City, the statue of King George III was torn down.

shoes had worn out on the long march. They immediately set to work building log shelters, which provided protection from the cold, damp winter weather. The men were given rations of meat and bread but often existed on "fire cake," a tasteless mixture of flour and water they cooked over open fires. Diseases such as typhoid, dysentery, and pneumonia spread through the camp. As many as 2,000 soldiers became sick and died.

Polly Cooper and the Oneida

A group of Oneida Indians, organized by Chief Shenandoah, brought 250 bushels of corn to help feed General Washington's army. Polly Cooper, an Oneida woman, taught them to make a corn soup that helped feed the starving soldiers. She remained with the army to help care for the men and refused to take any money for her work. The officers' wives took Polly shopping, and when she admired a shawl, they asked Congress to give them the money to buy it. The shawl remains a treasured artifact of the Oneida nation.

As the winter of 1777 set in, George Washington needed a winter refuge for his army. He chose Valley Forge, Pennsylvania, 18 miles (29 kilometers) from Philadelphia, because it was easy to defend against British attacks. On December 19, 1777, Washington's army of 12,000 men straggled into Valley Forge. They were poorly clothed and many were barefoot because their

Despite building log cabins for shelter, many Colonial soldiers became seriously ill during the long winter.

⊛ Valley Forge, Pennsylvania

THE ONEIDA HERITAGE

Many Oneida fought beside the Americans. They took part in the Battle of Oriskany on August 6, 1777, in which over 500 Oneida died. The battle proved a turning point in the war. Unfortunately, their support for the colonists alienated them from their former Iroquois Confederacy allies, who destroyed their main village and drove them from their traditional home. In 1794, the Oneida signed a treaty with the United States government that assured them protection over their lands in New York. The state of New York ignored the treaty and the land was reduced from 6 million acres (2.5 million hectares) to 32 acres (13 hectares). Many Oneida moved to Canada and Wisconsin. In 1974, the United States Supreme Court ruled that New York's actions were illegal, and that the Oneida could take action through the courts. Today, the Oneida continue to fight for their rights.

Baron Friedrich von Steuben

Baron Friedrich von Steuben

Baron Friedrich von Steuben was a Prussian drillmaster who came to Valley Forge to train the troops. He drilled them throughout the winter, teaching them to march in formation and cut the time it took to load and reload their guns. By the time the Continental Army paraded on May 6, 1778, they had transformed from ragged soldiers into a trained fighting force.

A NEW WAY TO SEE

Boston, Massachusetts, 1838

MORNING... Emma lay in bed, waiting for her mother to come and help her dress. She only knew it was morning because she'd heard the rooster crow. In her dark world, day and night were the same. The pink glow of a morning sky and the blazing red of sunset were distant memories from the days before she'd had scarlet fever nine years ago, at the age of three. The fever had stolen her sight, and now she could see only through the eyes of others, such as her brother, David, and her sister, Kathy. But David was newly married and living in his own house, and Kathy was too busy with parties and schoolwork to spend much time with Emma. And today Emma was leaving home. Her parents, Sarah and Gordon Riley, had enrolled her at the Perkins School for the Blind, a place where they taught children who are blind how to read, write, and become independent.

"Good morning, Emma." Her mother's cheery voice shook Emma from her thoughts. She sat up and held out her hands. Her mother grasped them. Emma noticed her hands felt as cold as her own.

Emma let her mother help her out of bed and shivered as she poured water over her hands from the pitcher on the washstand. She handed Emma a cloth to wipe her face. As her mother dressed her, Emma thought of the day ahead. After breakfast, she, her mother, and her father would ride to the school in the family's carriage. Her eyes filled with tears.

"I don't want to go," she shouted. "Why are you sending me away?"

"It is for your own good. You will learn to read and write and have friends who—"

"Who are blind like me? I want to stay here." Emma stamped her foot. "I want to be in my own bed, my own home!"

"Emma, we have always given in to you. You have been spoiled and pampered. But this time your father and I are standing firm. You *will* go to the Perkins School today, and that is that!"

Emma was stunned by the determination in her mother's voice. She would have to do as her parents dictated. What choice did she have? *I'll go*, she thought. *But I don't *have to like it!

The Perkins School for the Blind was housed in a stately brick building on Pearl Street in Boston. As they entered, Emma's mother described the wide entry hall with its wood paneling and the large, sunny room where they were asked to wait. Several minutes later they were shown into the director's office.

"Welcome to our school," said the director, Dr. Samuel Gridley Howe. "We are delighted to have you with us."

Emma didn't answer.

"We hope you will be happy here and take advantage of the educational opportunities we have to offer," said Dr. Howe. "And now, Emma, it is time to say goodbye to your parents." He rang a bell. Emma heard footsteps. "Caroline, this is Emma, our new student."

"Hello, Emma," said Caroline. "We are going to be roommates."

She placed Emma's hand on her arm. Emma's fingers touched soft cotton. From the sound of Caroline's voice, she decided that she was about fourteen years old.

"Goodbye, Emma." Mrs. Riley's voice was teary.

For a moment, Emma felt sorry for her mother; then her heart hardened and she turned away.

"Emma, please. I don't want to leave you like this."

You just want to leave me, Emma thought. She grasped Caroline's arm. "Take me to our room, please."

"Soon you will be able to find your way around the school all by yourself," Caroline said as Emma stumbled along beside her.

Emma doubted that. At home she relied on her family to take her from one room to the next. They showed her where to sit and even guided her hand as she ate. How would she ever learn to navigate this building that she'd been told was large, with three floors and many rooms? How could her parents do this to her? *How could they abandon her to strangers?*

Caroline seemed to read her mind. "I was angry, too, when my parents first brought me here. But now I know they wanted the best for me."

"How blind are you?" Emma asked skeptically.

"What do you mean?"

"Can you see at all?"

"A little," Caroline admitted. "I can make out shapes."

"I am in total darkness," said Emma, assured that her situation was far worse than that of her new roommate.

Caroline stopped walking and turned Emma around. Emma felt the other girl's warm breath on her face. "Emma, I know how frightening this is for you. But trust me. Dr. Howe has helped me and many others, and he will help you, too."

"Can he make me see?" Emma cried out.

"No," Caroline admitted. "But if you let him, he will help you learn how to be independent."

AFTERNOON... *My first meal here,* thought Emma. She sat on the bed in her new room and shuddered. Mealtime was an especially frightening experience. What would people think of her if she dribbled food down her chin or dripped it on her dress? *Well, they're blind, so at least they won't*

> *"I was angry, too, when my parents first brought me here. But now I know they wanted the best for me."*

see me. She giggled out loud. She had to admit that there was comfort in knowing that the other students shared her problems.

"Are you ready?" Caroline's voice interrupted her thoughts.

Emma stood. "Yes." She took a deep breath. She stepped forward, hesitated, and then took another step and bumped into something hard. "Ouch!" She touched her side. *I can't do this*, she thought.

"Here, let me help you." Caroline took her hand and guided her from the room. They walked down a long hallway and turned right. Caroline paused so that Emma could sense the space around her. "This is the dining room. There are long tables set in rows. "Walk forward ten steps and then turn to the right," she instructed. "Now stop. This is your place." She placed Emma's hand on the top of a chair, then pulled it out and helped Emma sit.

Wrapped in her blanket of darkness, Emma listened to the sounds in the room. She heard boys' and girls' voices, and older voices that must belong to teachers. The young voices sounded happy. Maybe Caroline was right. Maybe she *would* learn to like this place.

After lunch, Caroline took Emma to a room that she said was a classroom. "Emma, this is Miss Lydia Hall Drew. She's Dr. Howe's assistant, and she will teach you to read."

"Read! How can I read?" Emma demanded.

"You will learn to read using Dr. Howe's system of printing books with raised letters," said Miss Drew.

Emma listened to the woman's voice and tried to picture her. Miss Drew sounded younger than Dr. Howe but older than Emma. Miss Drew placed Emma's hand on her face.

"You can 'see' me with your fingertips," she said.

Emma felt Miss Drew's nose, her mouth, and her ears. "What color is your hair?"

"Brown."

"And your eyes?"

"Brown. Very boring," Miss Drew laughed.

Emma touched Miss Drew's face. "You feel pretty."

"Now feel your own face." Miss Drew guided Emma's hand. "You have lovely blue eyes. And your hair is the color of honey. You are very pretty."

"My sister, Kathy, is pretty. She goes to parties and dances."

"And you don't." Miss Drew's voice sounded sympathetic.

"People think that if you are blind, you are stupid," said Emma.

"Emma, you are not stupid. You can't see, but your brain is fine. There is someone I want you to meet." She took Emma's hand and wrapped it around a smaller hand. "Emma, this is Laura Bridgman. Laura came to our school last year. She had scarlet fever as an infant."

"Like me," said Emma.

"Yes. But the fever left Laura blind and deaf and unable to speak."

"How awful!" Emma tried to imagine being locked in a prison of darkness without sound. Her heart went out to this girl.

"When Laura first came here, she was terrified of everyone," said Caroline.

"Since then, Laura has learned to communicate with other people," said Miss Drew. "She did not even understand that common objects, such as forks and spoons, have names. She does now, and she has become Dr. Howe's star pupil."

"How old is Laura?" Emma asked.

"I will have her tell you." Miss Drew took Laura's hand and spelled out the question with her fingers. Laura took Emma's hand and tapped out the number eight.

"Is she eight years old? Did she tell me that she is eight years old?"

"That is right," said Miss Drew. "Dr. Howe and I have taught her to talk and listen with her fingers."

Caroline said, "You and I are lucky because we can both hear."

"What else have you taught Laura?" Emma asked Miss Drew.

Miss Drew placed Emma's hand on what felt like a piece of paper.

"What are those bumps?" Emma asked.

"They are letters. Together, they spell words. Dr. Howe's raised-letter system makes it possible for students who are blind to read."

Emma digested this information. "And you will teach me this system?"

"Yes," said Miss Drew. "We will start with simple things. First you must learn the letters of the alphabet. Then you will learn to connect letters to form words, and then to put words together to form sentences. Dr. Howe taught Laura words before letters because she needed to identify common objects. You have your hearing, so you already know many words."

"What about numbers?"

"You will learn the ten digits and then how to add them together to form larger numbers. Emma, your brain is a wondrous tool. You only have to unlock it from the darkness."

"Your mind is strong. Once you can read, the whole world will open to you. You will begin to ask questions and seek answers, and your spirit will come alive."

The word *darkness* soured Emma's mood. "I live in darkness," she said.

"Oh, but you need not." Miss Drew placed her hands on either side of Emma's head. "Your mind is strong. Once you can read, the whole world will open to you. You will begin to ask questions and seek answers, and your spirit will come alive." She stopped. "I do go on, don't I?"

"Yes, but I don't mind. Is Laura still here?"

"She is. Do you want to speak to her?"

Emma nodded.

Miss Drew placed Laura's hand in Emma's. "This is how you say hello." She moved Emma's fingers.

Laura responded. Emma beamed with delight.

"I want to tell her I am happy to meet her," said Emma.

"Like this." Again Miss Drew moved Emma's fingers and Laura responded.

"When Laura first came here, she couldn't communicate at all. People thought there was something wrong with her mind. But once she began to understand how to identify objects and read, she showed us how bright she really is. Now she is insatiable." Miss Drew paused. "Do you know what *insatiable* means?"

"No." Emma shook her head.

"It means that no matter how much she learns, she is never satisfied. She wants to know everything." Miss Drew laughed. "There is nothing wrong with Laura's brain, or with yours. It is a matter of putting them to work. Am I right, Caroline?"

"Yes." Caroline laughed. "You have certainly put my brain to work."

Emma heard the door open. She turned her head and recognized Dr. Howe's voice.

"Hello, Emma, Miss Drew. How is our newest pupil doing?"

"Hello, Dr. Howe." Emma suddenly remembered how rude she had been that morning. "Miss Drew has been teaching me to talk to Laura with my fingers."

"Good, good." Dr. Howe's voice was warm and enthusiastic. "Soon you will be reading raised-print books. I brought some with me from France and I have set up my own printing department to publish more."

"Will I learn everything, even mathematics, from your books?"

"No," Miss Drew said. "Dr. Howe uses different sizes of blocks to demonstrate the shapes of things and to teach mathematics." She took Emma's hand and placed it on a large round object.

"What is this?" Emma asked.

"It is a globe—a round ball with a map of the whole world. When you touch it, what do you feel?"

"The same kind of bumps I felt in the book."

"Yes. Once you can read those bumps, you will learn the names of countries all over the world."

"Miss Drew is an amazing teacher." Dr. Howe placed a hand on Emma's shoulder. "I will leave you now. You are in good hands."

Emma heard the door open and close. She turned to her teacher. "Miss Drew, can you really teach me to read?"

"Of course she can," said Caroline. "She will teach you to read and to write with a pencil and a special writing frame. The

system is called *square hand*. With it, you will be able to tell your parents about your life here."

At the mention of her parents, Emma felt sad. She had treated them badly that morning. They only wanted the best for her, but she had acted as if they were shutting her away in a tower. *Like a princess in a fairy tale*, she thought. Only here, there was no prince charming. She would be rescued by her own hard work and the skill of her teacher. Without thinking she reached out, took Laura's hand, and squeezed it. The other girl squeezed back, and then threaded her fingers through Emma's. The soft, childish touch was soothing.

If Laura can learn, so can I, Emma thought. *I can do this. I will do this.*

EVNING... Emma settled into the soft cushions of a sofa. She smoothed her skirt, the way her mother had taught her, and folded her hands in her lap. She felt the cushions shift as Caroline sat beside her. Around her, voices rose and fell as students and teachers in the parlor discussed the day's events. Footsteps told Emma that Dr. Howe was moving to the front of the room. He cleared his throat, and everyone stopped talking.

"Good evening. Before we start tonight's reading, I want to introduce our newest student, Emma Riley."

Emma smiled as the other students applauded. "Emma is twelve years old and is eager to learn all that we can teach her. I hope everyone will help her become adjusted to our school. Now, then." He opened a book. "Tonight I will read to you from *Pilgrim's Progress*, which I have just printed in embossed letters, or Boston Line Type." He cleared his throat and began.

As I walk'd through the wilderness of this world, I lighted on a certain place where was a Den, and I laid me down in that place to sleep; and as I slept, I dreamed a Dream…

Emma let her mind drift. It had been a long day and she was tired. Supper had been less of an ordeal than lunch. She had found her seat and, with Caroline's help, eaten her meal with only one spill of her soup. After dinner, Caroline had led her down the hall to another room on the first floor. "This is the parlor," she had explained as she helped Emma sit. "Dr. Howe will read to us and then we will hear music."

Emma loved music. Most nights after supper, her family gathered in the Rileys' parlor and listened to her mother play on their small spinet piano. Sometimes Father joined in on his banjo and they sang popular songs like "The Old Armchair" or "I've Been Working on the Railroad."

I've been working on the railroad, all the livelong day.

I've been working on the railroad, just to pass the time away.

Emma turned her head toward the music. This wasn't her memory. This was real—here in the Perkins School parlor. Everyone was singing, and after a brief hesitation, she joined in.

Can't you hear the whistle blowing, so early in the morn?

Can't you hear the captain shouting, "Dinah blow your horn"?

"You have a lovely voice," Caroline said. "Perhaps you will join the girls' choir."

Emma kept singing, but her mind was racing. *I will learn to read and write, do mathematics, and sing!* Again she felt a wave of shame over the way she had treated her parents that morning.

"Caroline, I want to tell my parents that I was wrong when I did not want to come here," Emma said when they were in their room preparing for bed.

"Tomorrow you will write them a letter."

"I can't write!"

"But you can talk, can you not? You will tell me what you want to say and I will write it for you."

"Would you? That will be wonderful." Emma clapped her hands. "Is that how you communicate with your family?"

"Yes. But my father must read my letters to my mother. You see," Caroline paused, "my mother is also blind."

Emma's mouth fell open. "She is?"

"Yes. I was born blind, as was my mother. Our doctor says it is probably something that is in our blood. No one knows why it happens."

"Did your mother attend the Perkins School when she was young?"

"No. The school did not exist back then. That is why she and my father were so happy to enroll me here. They said I would have an opportunity that my mother and others like her could only dream of. Maybe someday, everyone who's blind will have the same opportunity."

Caroline helped Emma put on her nightdress and wash up. Then she guided

Tomorrow I will start my new life. And the first thing I will do is write to my parents to thank them for insisting that I come here.

her to the bed.

"Tomorrow I will find my way to the dining room by myself," said Emma, as she stretched out and Caroline covered her with a quilt. She heard the springs squeak in the next bed.

"Caroline?" she called out softly.

"Yes?"

"I feel sorry for Laura because she can't hear the music."

"Oh, but she does. She hears it through her fingers, by picking up the vibrations."

"I want to get to know her."

"And you shall. Now go to sleep, Emma. Tomorrow you will have a busy day."

Yes, thought Emma. *Tomorrow I will start my new life. The first thing I will do is write to my parents to thank them for insisting that I come here.* Then she had another thought.

"Caroline?"

"Yes," answered a sleepy voice.

"Will Dr. Howe let me play the piano?"

"I imagine he will."

"Is there embossed music?"

"I do not think so. At least not yet."

"Then I will just pick out the tunes by memory."

"That will be wonderful. Good night."

"Good night, Caroline." Emma lay silent for a moment, and then called out, "Caroline, perhaps we can ask Dr. Howe to publish some songs in raised letters so others can play them, too."

She heard Caroline mutter something.

"What did you say?

"I said *insatiable*. Miss Drew said that once your mind is unlocked, you would want to know and do everything. I just did not think it would happen so fast."

Emma laughed aloud. "Insatiable. I like the sound of that. Caroline, are you insatiable, too?"

"Yes," mumbled Caroline. "Now, *please*, Emma, go to sleep."

And with a sigh of contentment, Emma did just that. ✪

A NEW WAY TO SEE
The Perkins School for the Blind

In August 1832, the New England Asylum for the Blind opened its doors in Boston, Massachusetts. Its director, Samuel Gridley Howe, wanted to open an institution where blind and deaf-blind children could get an education and learn to care for themselves.

He convinced his father to convert his home into a school, which quickly grew to have sixty students. A wealthy merchant, Colonel Thomas H. Perkins, donated his large house on Pearl Street for the expanded school. By 1839, that house was so overcrowded that Perkins allowed the school to sell it and buy a hotel building in South Boston. In his honor, the school was eventually named the Perkins School.

A New Way to Read

In Europe, Howe saw a system of raised type. This allowed blind people to use their sense of touch to read. He brought back books, maps, and diagrams to America and created his own materials from pasteboard, gummed twine, and pins. He used blocks of different sizes to teach mathematical proportions. Students used pasted string to learn about geometric figures, and they studied geography on a large globe with raised features. Howe started his own printing department to produce books with raised type. This system became known as Boston Line Type. Author Charles Dickens was so impressed by this work, he wrote about it in his book *American Notes* and also had the school print 250 copies of his book *The Old Curiosity Shop* in Boston Line Type.

The Work Continues

The Perkins School continued to grow and develop. In 1880, it opened a library on blindness and deafness. A few years later, it opened the first American kindergarten for blind children. Over the years, the Perkins School has expanded to work with sighted children with other disabilities, such as cerebral palsy, deafness, and learning disabilities, and with visually impaired elders. The school trains teachers, and it partners internationally with hundreds of agencies to provide training and services to blind people worldwide.

Boston, Massachusetts

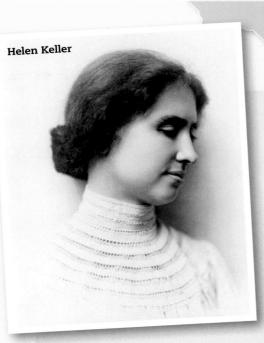

Helen Keller

A PLACE IN HISTORY

THE PERKINS SCHOOL'S FAME SPREADS AROUND THE WORLD

Howe's success with seemingly "unteachable" deaf-blind students made him and the school famous. One early deaf-blind student, Laura Bridgman, was taught to use her sense of touch to communicate: first with individual letters, then by connecting the letters into words, and finally by connecting the words to objects. After only two months, Laura had a breakthrough.

Perkins's best-known student was Helen Keller, a blind-deaf child whose mother read about the school in Dickens's *American Notes*. Michael Anagnos, who had taken over after Howe's death, sent Annie Sullivan to tutor Helen at her home in Alabama. In the beginning, Helen fought Annie's attempts to teach her. But Annie persisted. Once Helen learned to finger spell, her natural intelligence blossomed. Helen later graduated from Radcliffe College and became a world-famous advocate for people with disabilities.

A GOLD NUGGET FOR ADAM

Sacramento, California, 1855

MORNING... Adam Parnum stepped out of his tent, blinked, and stretched. Another day in the muddy gold fields. Did his father really think they would strike it rich? They had been here for over six months, and all they had to show for their efforts were callused hands and sore backs.

"Mornin', Son." His father looked up from where he was frying bacon over an open fire. "Good day for prospectin' gold."

"Good day for catching cold." Adam looked up at the gray March sky and shivered. "My overalls are soaked, Pa. How am I supposed to work like this?"

His father took the frying pan off the fire and set it on the ground. "When we strike gold, you can buy all the overalls you want."

When we strike gold! Adam tried to contain his anger. Striking gold was his father's answer to everything. And he was tired of it. He was tired of being a "Forty-niner," as the prospectors were called. That was because most of them had come here in 1849. The Parnums were latecomers.

When they'd set out from St. Louis for the gold fields, Adam had been excited. What an adventure! All they had to do was stake a claim and pick gold nuggets from the ground. The reality was far different from the dream. In the first days after Mr. James Wilson Marshall discovered gold on the American River, the prospectors who flocked there found gold in the riverbeds and lying on the ground. They had only to stoop down and pick it up. Later, miners panned for gold, a process that separated the river dirt from the metal ore. By the time Adam and his father arrived, mining had become hard work, digging into rock. Only a lucky few were striking it rich. Still, Sam Parnum held on to his dream.

There were two ways to get to California: by sea or overland along the Oregon–California Trail. His father had chosen the overland trail. His mother, Louisa, had helped outfit a covered wagon with supplies. "Our whole life savings is going into this venture," she had said, as Sam and Adam piled sacks of flour and beans, barrels of salt pork, coffee and sugar, a tent, and mining pans into the wagon.

"You and the boys keep the farm running," Sam said. He picked her up and whirled her around. "When we return you'll be wearin' gold from head to toe."

Louisa had looked unconvinced but held her tongue. If her husband believed in this venture, then it was her duty to support his dream. That her oldest son was going with him calmed her nerves. She told Adam that she was counting on him to keep his father out of trouble. At the time, Adam had not known what she meant. Now he understood that the pressures of the mining camps often turned men to drink and gambling.

Adam took a plate from his father. Beans and bacon—that was all they ever ate. Occasionally they would get freshly baked bread from one of the women who ran a kitchen in the camp. Adam's mouth watered for his mother's savory stews and fruit pies. As he ate, he thought about their dilemma. They had spent all their money getting to the gold fields. Once here, his father had staked out a claim, but it was yet to pay off. The little gold they found barely covered the cost of food. He knew that many of the Forty-niners got sick, and some died. Others gave up and either begged their way home or stayed for lack of money to leave. He did not want that to happen to them.

They had spent all their money getting to the gold fields. Once here, his father had staked out a claim, but it was yet to pay off. The little gold they found barely covered the cost of food.

"Eat up, Son. We haven't got all day."

Adam scooped up the last of the beans and handed his father his plate. He stood and stretched. Working the claim was hard on the body. It meant digging and scooping out dirt. His back, arms, and shoulders ached. As he looked at his father, Adam thought how much he had aged. His once-dark hair was streaked with gray and his skin was dry as shoe leather. The gold fields did that to a man. Adam wondered what he would look like to his mother and two younger brothers. He was fourteen but felt older.

"Let's go," his father said.

Feigning an enthusiasm he did not feel, Adam shouldered his pick and shovel and followed his father out of the camp and up the mountain trail to their claim.

Adam picked up the pan he was using to prospect for gold. He mixed dirt with water and gently shook the pan back and forth so the lighter dirt would wash away, leaving the gold at the bottom. He looked into the pan. No gold. He sighed. Beside him, his father was working the long tom. It was a box slightly longer than the height of an adult man and built like a cradle. His father shoveled dirt into it, then poured water over the dirt and rocked the tom. Up and down the river, Adam saw other miners doing the same thing.

"*Hola,* Adam. *Que paso?*"

Adam looked up as his friend Miguel Torres walked by. Miguel was here with his father, too, but unlike the Parnums, the Torreses were not miners. They made money selling supplies to the miners.

"Look at my new overalls." Miguel stood legs apart, hands in his pockets. "They're called waist overalls. See, they are made of strong fabric and have pockets that do not tear when you put gold nuggets or tools in them. I bought them in San Francisco."

Adam tried to hide his envy. Miguel and his father often went to San Francisco to pick up the supplies they sold to the miners. Miguel entertained Adam with stories of that great city 150 miles southwest of the gold fields. Each time he returned with new clothing and tales of the bustling seaport with its rows of stores and saloons.

"The overalls look comfortable." Adam fingered the twilled cotton cloth. It was softer than the canvas material of his overalls, yet strong and durable.

Adam watched jealously as Miguel sauntered away. He was happy to have him as a friend—there were few enough people his age in the gold fields—yet he wished Miguel would stop showing off. He picked up his pan, scooped up more dirt and water, and started shaking it gently back and forth. The motion was hypnotic and his mind wandered. *What were his brothers doing? How was the farm? How was his mother managing without them?* His father's shout startled him from his reverie.

"Eureka! You've struck gold!"

"What?" Adam stared into his pan. There on the bottom, shining like a miniature sun, was the biggest gold nugget he had ever seen.

All along the river, miners dropped their pans and left their long toms to crowd around Adam and his father.

"What is in your pan, *muchacho?*"

Adam looked up into the dark eyes of Señor Torres, Miguel's father.

"Gold!" Mr. Parnum crowed. He poked Adam's arm. "My boy struck gold!"

Adam proudly held out his pan. "How much do you think it is worth, Señor Torres?"

Señor Torres picked up the nugget. He bounced it in his hand. "You must have it weighed at the assayer's office, but it is big and will probably bring you much money. Be careful. You do not want to lose it."

AFTERNOON... "We've got to get this to the assayer's office," said Adam as he and his father headed back to the mining camp. "Now we'll have the money to go home." He touched the leather pouch at his waist, where he'd deposited his find.

"Go home!" His father whirled around to face him. "This is our first good strike. We can buy supplies and stake ourselves out for months."

"No! I think we should take our money and bring it home to Ma."

"Your ma's doing just fine. She can wait another few months for us."

"How do you know that? We haven't had a letter since Christmas." Adam kicked the ground in exasperation. "Pa, this was lucky, but it doesn't mean it'll happen again. We need to go home."

His father turned his steely gray eyes on him. "I ain't a quitter, boy. There's a fortune to be made in them gold fields, and I intend to stay here and do it."

There on the bottom, shining like a miniature sun, was the biggest gold nugget he had ever seen.

"Gold fever," Adam muttered as they resumed walking. His father had caught the most contagious disease in the camp—greed!

The walk back was cold and muddy. Adam looked at the walls of rock, each a potential repository of unfound gold. *We could stay here forever*, he thought. He knew some miners were making California their home. Others had died from disease or hunger and were buried in these mountains. Neither option appealed to Adam. Why didn't his father see that their future lay in the fertile fields of Missouri, not in the mountains of California?

Back in camp, Adam went into their tent and stretched out on his bedroll. He was exhausted. His father had gone to the saloon to have a drink to celebrate their good luck. Adam wanted to rest before starting the long walk to the assay office. He closed his eyes and, with his hand clutching the leather pouch, drifted off to sleep.

Was it a sound or movement that woke him? Lifting his head, he waited for his eyes to focus in the dim light of the tent. He was alone but something felt wrong. His hand flew to his hip. The leather pouch was gone!

Adam jumped to his feet and flew out of the tent. Where was his father? Had Pa taken the pouch? And if he had, would their treasure be safe in a den of men drinking and gambling? Especially with his father's fondness for poker?

The day was dark with a rumble of thunder coming over the mountains. Adam raced through the camp, barely acknowledging the greetings of the miners as he went. When he reached the saloon, he paused. He had never been inside before. This was a place for men, not boys. He knew what went on inside—whiskey, gambling, and fights that often broke out among desperate men who were far from home. Taking a deep breath, he pushed through the swing doors and entered.

The room was blue with tobacco smoke. Men sat at tables and lounged against the bar. Most were miners. He could tell from their weary faces and work worn hands. He searched the crowd. Where was his father? He spotted him at a table in the back of the room. Pushing through the crowd, Adam planted his feet beside his father's chair.

"Where is it?"

"Where is what?" Mr. Parnum looked up at his son in surprise.

"My pouch. With the gold nugget inside."

His father gave him a puzzled look. "It's tied to your belt."

"That's what I'm trying to tell you. It's not there."

"It probably fell off in the tent. Go look for it."

Adam looked at the cards and piles of silver dollars on the table. "Pa, have you lost it in this poker game?"

"How can I lose something I don't have?" His father turned back to the table. "Now leave me be."

"Scat, sonny," said one of the miners. "You're disturbing a friendly game of poker."

"As friendly as that game when my father lost our horses?" Adam wanted to punch the man in the face but controlled himself. "Where is it?" Adam demanded. He swept his hand across the table, brushing the cards and stacks of coins onto the floor.

"Now you hold it there, boy." A bearded man wearing a battered felt hat grabbed Adam's arm. "I don't care whose son you are, you can't come in here disruptin' our game."

By now a crowd had gathered. Adam was overwhelmed by the angry roar of the miners.

"What's goin' on here?" Will Crawford, the self-appointed sheriff of the camp, stepped into the fray. "Who's causin' this ruckus?"

"These two." The man in the hat pointed at Adam and his father. "I think it's time they left."

The sheriff stepped up to Mr. Parnum. "Why don't you troublemakers mosey out of here before these 'uns," he jerked his thumb at the crowd, "go for the tar and feathers."

"It's a sad state of affairs when a man can't enjoy a friendly poker game." said Mr. Parnum as he crammed his hat on his head and stalked to the door. Adam followed closely behind him.

"I was winning that game," Mr. Parnum growled when they were outside.

"I thought you'd taken the nugget to gamble with, and I didn't want you to lose it." Adam's face was flushed. "But if you really don't have it..." his voice trembled, "we've been robbed."

"Robbed!" his father exploded. "I left that nugget with *you*! To keep it *safe*!" His face was purple. He raised a hand to slap Adam. Adam sidestepped in anticipation of the blow.

"Fighting isn't going to get our gold back!" he cried.

His father dropped his hand. "It's too late. It's gone," he sighed. "Whoever took that nugget is probably in 'Frisco by now."

EVENING... The mood around the campfire was somber. Adam sat cross-legged, staring into the flames while his father fried up the last of their bacon. Neither was hungry. Usually, other miners would stop by to offer greetings and compare the day's results. But tonight, no one came. Adam looked up as his father handed him a plate.

"Pa, can I ask you a question?"

"Depends on what it is." Mr. Parnum squatted next to him. He stared into the fire, as if looking for a message in the flames.

"If you did have the nugget...I mean, if you had been the one to take it from me..." Adam swallowed. "...would you have...?"

"Would I have gambled it away?" His father slammed his fist into the palm of his hand. "I don't know!" he cried. He jumped to his feet and paced back and forth. "I've been asking myself the same question. Truth is, Son, I just don't know."

"But you might have."

"Yeah, I reckon I might have." He squatted on his heels next to Adam. "I'm not proud to say it, but that's the way it is with me."

"You weren't like that at home." Adam studied his father. "Why did you change?"

A slow smile split his father's leathery face. "At home I had your ma to keep my

Where was his father? Had Pa taken the pouch? And if he had, would their treasure be safe in a den of men drinking and gambling?

feet on the ground. This is a wild place. No women, no families."

"I'm family." Adam fought back tears. "Ain't I your family, Pa?"

"That you are." His father placed a hand on Adam's shoulder.

They finished eating in silence. Adam took their plates to the stream to wash up. When he came back, his father had gone into the tent. Adam sat by the smoldering fire. A rustling sound made him jump to his feet. Whirling around, he found himself staring at Miguel.

Miguel put a finger to his lips, reached into his pocket, and pulled out a leather pouch. "I have something that is yours."

Adam stared at him in surprise. "*You* took the pouch! You came into the tent while I was sleeping?"

Miguel nodded. "I was very quiet, wasn't I?"

"Why?"

"So you can take it to the assayer's office in the morning."

Adam stared at him. "That doesn't make any sense. You stole it from us and now you're giving it back?"

Miguel squatted beside Adam. "My father told me to do it."

"I must explain for my son." Señor Torres approached. He took the pouch from his son and handed it to Adam.

Adam opened it and looked inside. "The nugget is here."

"Of course," said Señor Torres. "My son is not a thief."

"Now I make money selling pots and pans to the miners. But soon I will have enough so that Miguel and I can go home and open a store. You and your father should learn from my mistakes."

Behind them, the tent flap opened and Mr. Parnum appeared. "Torres! What on Earth are you doing here at this time of night?" he bellowed.

"Pa, they came to return our gold."

Mr. Parnum looked from Adam to Miguel and then to Señor Torres. "You *took* it?"

Señor Torres held up a hand. "Please. Let me explain."

"I reckon you oughta," Mr. Parnum said, his voice shaking.

"Six years ago, when I came here with my wife and son from Mexico, the gold was on the ground. Many people made fortunes—one, two, three thousand dollars a day. I did, too. But I gambled my money away. My wife took our baby daughter and returned to Mexico. But I stayed, and Miguel stayed with me."

"My father told me to take the nugget so your father would not lose it in a card game," said Miguel.

"I see that the gambling streak is strong in your father," Señor Torres said with a pause. "As it was with me." He faced Adam. "And I see the home streak is strong in you. Take the money from your bonanza and go home."

"But you didn't leave."

"No." Señor Torres smiled ruefully. "Now I make money selling pots and pans to the miners. But soon I will have enough that Miguel and I can go home and open a store. You and your father can learn from my mistakes."

Adam turned to his father. "Pa?"

Mr. Parnum took a menacing step toward Señor Torres. "I should beat you to a pulp." He looked as if he would explode. His body stiffened and his eyes glittered with rage. Then he breathed a deep sigh and his body slumped. "But I won't because you are right."

He held out his hand. Señor Torres grasped it and the two men shook.

Adam and Miguel remained by the fire after their fathers left. Adam watched as a puff of sparks exploded into the night air.

"How soon will you go back to your home?" asked Miguel.

"We will need to get a wagon and supplies. And horses," Adam added, recalling the two his father had lost in a poker game. "I hope the nugget gives us enough money."

"My father says it will. We will help you get supplies." Miguel stared up at the sky. "The stars are beautiful. Here in the mountains I feel much closer to the heavens," he said.

"There are no mountains in Missouri." Adam poked the fire with a stick. "I will miss them. I will miss you, too."

"We will be far apart, but we will still be *amigos*," said Miguel.

"Si." Adam smiled. Then, as Miguel turned to go, he said, "The next time you go to San Francisco, can I come with you?"

"Si. Why?

Adam pointed to Miguel's overalls. "To buy waist overalls, to take to Missouri."

"To wear or to sell?"

"Maybe both," Adam grinned. "I think farmers would like to wear overalls that don't fall down. My mother can sew them and I will sell them."

"And I will sell you the fabric," said Miguel, nodding.

"We will be partners," Adam laughed. And with a final good night, he went into the tent, lay down on his blanket, and fell fast asleep. ✪

A GOLD NUGGET FOR ADAM
The California Gold Rush

In January 1848, James Wilson Marshall discovered gold near Sacramento, California. When a successful storekeeper named Sam Brannan came to San Francisco with a bottle filled with gold dust, he started a wild rush that brought thousands of people to that part of California. In August 1848, *The New York Herald* printed a story about gold. Suddenly, people from all over the United States joined the gold prospectors. Some traveled in covered wagons over the mountains; others went by the longer sea routes, either to Panama or around Cape Horn and then up the Pacific coast. These people were called Forty-niners because most of them came in 1849. Dozens of mining camps sprung up and turned the small town of San Francisco into a thriving city.

Later prospectors sorted through endless piles of rocks with no guarantee of finding gold.

A Difficult Quest

The early prospectors had an easy time finding gold. All they had to do was use a knife to pry it out of rocks or shovel sand and river dirt into a metal dish and swirl it around. Since gold is heavier than dirt it would sink to the bottom of the pan. When the sand and water was poured off, any rocks and gold stayed behind. But this easy gold soon ran out. Later miners had to dig deeper into rocks and under riverbeds—many did not find any gold at all. In the end, about 400,000 miners came to the gold fields from all over the world. The mining camps were basic and food was scarce. Also, sickness and disease were very common.

Underground mines were dug to try to find gold beneath the surface.

Sacramento,
California

GOLD BUYS CALIFORNIA A PLACE IN THE UNION

The gold rush was a major reason California became a state. The United States acquired California in 1848 as part of the settlement after the Mexican War. At the time, there was a lot of debate about whether President Polk should have taken California from Mexico. But once gold was discovered, the next president, Zachary Taylor, pushed to make California a state. No one knows how much treasure was taken from the gold fields, but some guess it was as much $48 million! Even though some people went home after the gold rush, many stayed and set up permanent homes in California. The combination of lots of money and many new people changed California's history and brought the borders of the United States all the way to the Pacific Ocean.

Panning for gold in a river was easy, but often unsuccessful.

A BOY WITH A DRUM

Gainesville, Virginia, 1862

MORNING... Samuel put on his hat, straightened his tunic, and picked up his drum. Then he stepped from the tent. It was still dark, but the camp was in motion. General John Pope's army was going to attack the Confederate soldiers who were holed up in a railroad excavation across the field. All around the camp, soldiers were eating breakfast, cleaning their guns, and waiting for the order to begin the fight. Samuel shivered. Today he would be part of the battle.

A tall man in a blue Union Army uniform approached him. "Good morning, Samuel. Are you ready to fight?"

"Yes sir, Captain Bradshaw." Samuel saluted as he had been taught. *I may be only twelve, but I know how to act like a real soldier,* he thought. *I am a real soldier.*

Samuel had enlisted in the Union Army along with his brother, Andrew, who was 18. His chest swelled with pride. Captain Bradshaw had chosen him from among the many drummer boys in the camp. His job was to act as an orderly for the captain. He carried water, rubbed down the captain's horse, gathered wood for fires, and helped cook the captain's meals. In battle, it was his job to beat out commands on his drum. That meant walking in front of the troops, which he knew was very dangerous. Many drummer boys were killed. In spite of the risk, Samuel wanted to be here. *I am doing something important for my country,* he thought, repressing a sudden urge to turn and run away. He glanced to the east, where wisps of clouds streaked with pink heralded the new day. Squaring his shoulders, he turned back to the captain. "We are going to beat those Johnny Rebs, are we not?"

Captain Bradshaw rubbed his chin. It was covered with soft brown stubble. "I hope so, son," he said. "I do hope so." The captain then left to continue readying his troops for the day's fighting.

Samuel turned to a nearby soldier. "What does he mean, 'I hope so'?"

> "Don't get too cocky, young man. Remember, this is a battle, and people are gonna shoot at you. You be on your guard."

"Well, sonny, the captain is remembering the last time our army came to this very field." He pushed back his hat and ran a hand across his brow. "Beat the pants off us, the Rebs did. This time it's gonna be different. I heard the captain say that General Stonewall Jackson has led his men into a trap."

"Sure did," said a second soldier. "Yesterday he attacked our column as we marched along the Warrenton Turnpike. Then he pulled back and led his men down into an abandoned railroad grade." He grinned, revealing tobacco-stained teeth. "Old Stonewall is in for a surprise. There's no way out of that ravine. We'll storm their position, and they'll have to surrender or be killed."

Samuel's eyes shone. "I will beat my drum so loud that our troops will hear me to the last man."

The soldier gave him a warning look. "Don't get too cocky, young man. Remember, this is a battle, and people are gonna shoot at you. You be on your guard."

"That is good advice. You'd best heed it, Samuel."

"Andrew!" Samuel turned at the sound of his brother's voice. "What do you think about the battle?"

"I am wary of underestimating the great Stonewall Jackson."

"Andrew, why do the Confederates call their general Stonewall?"

"I can answer that," said the first soldier. "In July 1861, during the first Battle of Bull Run, General Jackson's army blocked our advance. His soldiers said that he was as strong as a *stone wall,* so that is what they call him."

"Will he block us this time?" asked Samuel.

"No, young man. They have retreated into an indefensible location. We will win."

"Of course we will." Samuel grinned. "Can I carry a musket instead of a drum?"

Andrew cuffed Samuel's ear. "There's going to be plenty of time for guns when you are older. Your job today is to drum the men into battle."

Something about the word *battle* made Samuel's smile disappear. *People will be shooting at us. I might be killed,* he thought. He looked up at Andrew. "Are you afraid?"

"Of course I am." Andrew smiled at him kindly. "It is all right to be frightened, Samuel. The important thing is not to let the fear rule you once the fighting begins." He clapped a hand on Samuel's shoulder. "Come," he said, "the general is addressing the troops."

General Pope stood before his men. His dark blue uniform was pressed and his posture was ramrod straight. The soldiers stood at attention waiting for his instructions. "This is an important battle," he said in a voice that carried to the farthest corner of the field. "The fate of the nation rests on our shoulders. Today we will show the Rebels that they are no match for the Union Army."

Samuel listened to the general's speech with pride. His father had taught him the meaning of this war. The South had seceded from the United States. The North was fighting to preserve the Union and keep the country together. Samuel's family lived in Pennsylvania. His father, Abraham Cooper, was a farmer and a fervent abolitionist. He believed that slavery was an evil, and that the practice must be ended. If the South won the war, he had said, the Union would be torn apart and slavery would continue. Elliott Washington, a former slave who worked on the farm, had told Samuel stories of whippings and slave auctions where children were wrenched from the arms of their mothers. *My father cannot fight because he is too old, but Andrew and I will help to win this war for him. We are doing God's work,* Samuel thought.

"Samuel!" Captain Bradshaw's voice cut through his thoughts. "Ready your drum! We are going into battle."

Rat-a-tat-tat. Rat-a-tat-tat. Samuel beat out the rhythm to keep the column moving. Beside him, a row of drummer boys tapped out the same staccato cadence. They were at the front of the line with thousands of men following. The day was hot, and Samuel's skin itched from the sweat under his uniform. He looked across the field to the railroad embankment. From there the land dipped into the deep cut where Stonewall Jackson's soldiers were holed up.

The drummers' beating intensified as the column of Union soldiers moved closer to the embankment. Then Samuel saw a line of gray emerging over the edge of the ravine. The line became a wave as thousands of Confederate soldiers rose from the hole and swarmed onto the field. It was Samuel's job to warn the soldiers at the rear of the impending attack. He hit his drum with all his strength. The other drummers did the same as Union soldiers pushed forward to meet the oncoming rush of Confederates.

For a moment, Samuel felt time stop as he watched two armies, blue and gray, race toward each other across a flat farmer's field. And then he heard it—the terrifying rebel yell: *Aayee-aay-eee*—as the Confederate soldiers charged. Horses neighed in terror. The ground shook from the boom of artillery shells. The boy beside him fell as a bullet pierced his tunic.

Samuel fought to remain upright as soldiers from both sides rushed past with guns firing and bayonets extended. He drummed harder. *What good is my drumming?* he thought as the noise of battle roared around him. His heart pounded; his ears felt like they would explode from the blast of artillery and the rebel yell: *Aayee-aay-eee!*

He kept moving, pounding his drum— *Rat-a-tat-tat! Rat-a-tat-tat!*—until suddenly he was sprawled on the ground. *Have I been hit?* He checked his uniform for blood. *I haven't been shot.* And then he saw the body. He had tripped over a Confederate soldier who lay dead with a hole in his chest.

Samuel struggled to his feet. He could not take his eyes off the dead soldier. No matter that his uniform was gray; he was a young man, only a few years older than Samuel himself.

"Why are you standing here, boy?! MOVE!!" An unknown hand pushed him forward. He stumbled around another body, this one wearing blue. He stopped and looked frantically around. *My drum! Where is my drum?* Turning, he tried to run back to where he had fallen, but the surge of battle pushed him onward. Panic stricken, he searched the field. And then he saw the abandoned musket.

AFTERNOON...

The tide of battle had turned. Instead of rolling over Stonewall Jackson's troops, General Pope's troops were now on the run. The weak entrapped army they had expected was instead a body of thousands of men that pushed them back with the force of a hurricane. As the Union soldiers retreated, they left a trail of dead, in blue and in gray. Samuel clutched his musket. Could he fire it? Could he actually put a bullet into another human being? He stumbled along, heart pounding, eyes on the ground. Where in this chaos was Andrew? Where was his unit? How had he ended up by himself, surrounded by enemy soldiers?

"Put down the musket!"

Samuel turned so fast his ankle twisted and he almost lost his balance. Before him was a boy about his age in a gray uniform.

"Drop the musket," the boy repeated.

Instead, Samuel lifted his gun. Now the two of them were faced off like opponents in a duel. The other boy cocked his gun. Samuel noticed his hand was trembling. *He is as scared as I am.* Samuel gasped for breath; his heart pounded and sweat streamed down his face. He lifted his head and stared into the boy's eyes. His gaze—a mixture of fear and daring—reminded Samuel of a fox he had once trapped in the woods. The fox had challenged him,

and admiring its bravery, Samuel had let it go. But not this time! Samuel pointed his gun and fired. The shot was wide and missed his opponent, who tried to fire back, failed, and then turned and ran away.

Samuel stared after him. *Why are we trying to kill each other?* Suddenly, the battle seemed to Samuel a terrible waste of life. Turning, he trudged along the path of retreat and then broke into a run. Faster and faster he ran, until a hand reached out and caught him.

"Put down the weapon, son."

Out of fear, Samuel tried to keep running. But the man's grip was firm. "Soldier!" Samuel looked up to see where the voice had come from. It belonged to a man wearing a blue uniform. "Calm down, son. I need you to help with the wounded."

Samuel stopped. He was still clutching his gun. His breathing slowed in relief.

"Are you a drummer boy?" the man asked him.

"Yes, sir."

"Good. I am a medic. You can help carry a stretcher."

Samuel relinquished his musket and followed the medic. The man's uniform was spattered with blood. He led Samuel to the far end of the field, where rows of men lay on the ground. Some were on stretchers. Others sat, heads in hands, shoulders slumped in defeat.

"We need all the hands we can find," said the medic.

Samuel looked at the sea of bodies, praying that Andrew was not among them. "What should I do?"

"We have to move these soldiers from the battlefield. Come over here. Help the orderlies carry these stretchers." Then the

50

medic moved off to tend to the next group of wounded men.

General Pope's army was in full retreat. Samuel watched as soldiers who only hours before had strutted with confidence now shuffled forward, heads bent and eyes downcast. He searched the crowd for Andrew but did not see him. "Where are we going?" he asked the man on the other end of the stretcher he was carrying. On it a soldier was moaning in pain.

"Back to Bull Run, more'n likely. Same as last time we fought here." The soldier shook his head. "They beat the pants off of us that time and they've done it again. Those Johnny Rebs ain't gonna let us lick 'em easy, that's for sure."

The retreat continued. From the front of the lines, Samuel heard the steady beat of the drummers, urging the men to keep moving. *Aayee-aay-ee!!* Like a raging storm, Stonewall Jackson's army lashed out at Pope's retreating troops.

"Listen to that whoop," said the soldier. "This war ain't gonna be over anytime soon. Not with them savages on our tail."

Samuel thought of the boy with the gun. *He is not a savage any more than I am a savage.* Once again he thought, *Why are we trying to kill each other?*

EVENING...

The Union Army regrouped at Bull Run under a pall of defeat so thick, it seemed to suck the air from the sky. All around Samuel, men mourned the day's losses. As they had retreated, General Pope had organized a group of soldiers to fight off the advancing Rebels in order to protect the rest of the army. It was this rearguard action that prevented a total defeat. Yet with thousands of men dead or wounded, it was impossible to think of the battle as anything other than a disaster.

Captain Bradshaw approached Samuel. "Is there news of your brother?"

"No, sir." Samuel saluted. "I pray that he has survived."

"I shall pray for him, as well as all our men." The captain walked off to speak with the next group of soldiers. Samuel's gaze followed his officer. For a moment, he just stood. It was all too much to understand. It had happened so fast.

"Samuel! Thank the Lord that you have survived."

"Andrew!" Samuel turned to his brother's voice. "You too were not killed!"

"It will take more than a Rebel's bullet to stop me." Andrew laughed but his eyes remained serious. "And how did you fare in the battle?"

Samuel looked his brother in the eyes. "I beat my drum, and later, when I lost it, I picked up a musket..." His voice broke.

"And...?" Andrew eyed him with close curiosity. "What did you then do with your musket?"

"I shot at a Rebel, but I missed. He tried to shoot me, but his gun misfired and he ran away." Samuel looked at the ground. "I let him go."

Andrew motioned for him to sit. "Samuel, you are not a coward because you

> *He is not a savage any more than I am a savage. Once again he thought, Why are we trying to kill each other?*

did not shoot at a retreating soldier. It is not easy to shoot another human being."

"But they are our enemies," Samuel said, his voice filled with misery.

Andrew pointed to a group of men gathered around a campfire. "Come. You should eat something."

Samuel and Andrew sat down in the circle around the campfire. Someone handed Samuel a plate of beans and salt pork. Suddenly, he was ravenous. He spooned the beans into his mouth while voices buzzed around him.

Stonewall sure threw us a surprise party.

He was lucky. Next time, we'll whip those Rebs.

It's their yell that curdles my blood. Never heard anything like it.

Never want to again.

You will. That yell is going to haunt us.

They want to scare us.

They sure did that! I thought the devil himself was comin' after me.

"I shot at a Rebel, but I missed. He tried to shoot me, but his gun misfired and he ran away." Samuel looked at the ground. "I let him go."

Samuel scooped the last of his food and stood. "I want to see how the man I carried is doing."

Andrew nodded.

As Samuel crossed the camp, his mind filled with images and he heard again the roar of the artillery, the shouts of men, and that terrifying rebel yell. When he entered the medic's tent a sour smell of sickness made him gag. Covering his mouth and nose with his hand, he walked down the row of cots filled with wounded soldiers. Some were sitting and greeted him as he passed. Others lay still as death. Samuel saw men with bandaged limbs and bruised and bloodied faces. Trying to ignore the groans and cries of pain, he continued until he found the soldier he had carried. He was sitting up, a tin plate of food on his lap.

Samuel held out his hand. "I helped bring you back from the battlefield."

"Thank you, son." He grasped Samuel's hand. "My name's Tom. Tom Cousins."

"I am Samuel Cooper. I am very happy that you were not killed."

"Me, too." Tom touched the bandage on his head. "Only a flesh wound. I may not be so lucky next time."

"I hope you are even luckier," Samuel said. "Please take care of yourself."

"You too, son. You drummer boys have the worst of the lot, bein' up front like shooting targets. Good luck to you," he saluted as Samuel turned to leave.

Outside the tent, Samuel took deep breaths. After the suffocating smells inside, the warm night air was like velvet caressing his throat. He was drawn to the sound of singing. He followed it to a campfire where a group of soldiers sat in a circle. Their voices rose to the sky.

Mine eyes have seen the glory of the coming of the Lord;

He is trampling out the vintage where the grapes of wrath are stored;

He hath loosed the fateful lightning of His terrible swift sword,

His truth is marching on.

Samuel joined the circle. "What is this song?" he asked a soldier.

"*The Battle Hymn of the Republic.* A lady named Julia Ward Howe wrote it. She didn't like the original lyrics."

"And what were they?" asked Samuel.

"Something about John Brown's body in

his grave. Miss Howe said they were awful words for such a beautiful melody. I read that in a newspaper."

"Did you find your soldier?" Andrew sat beside Samuel.

"Yes. He is well. But so many others are not."

"This war will get worse before it ends." Andrew said. He turned his head. "Julia Ward Howe wrote this song to inspire our troops."

"We will need inspiration, won't we?" asked Samuel.

"Yes, I am afraid we will."

"Andrew, I lost my drum in the battle."

"You will get another."

Samuel paused. "Andrew, I am frightened."

"We all are." Andrew patted his shoulder.

"Andrew, I want to write a letter to Ma and Pa. What should I say?"

"Tell them that you are well and serving the Union bravely, and that you hope to come home soon."

"And about you? Should I tell them the same thing?"

"Yes, Samuel. Tell them that we will both soon be home." Under his breath, Andrew whispered, "I pray this is true."

Around them soldiers' voices rose soft and hopeful into the night.

I have seen Him in the watch-fires of a hundred circling camps;

They have builded Him an altar in the evening dews and damps;

I can read His righteous sentence by the dim and flaring lamps,

His day is marching on.

Samuel joined the singing.

Glory, glory, hallelujah,

His truth is marching on.

And so am I, Samuel thought. *So am I.* ✪

A BOY WITH A DRUM
The Battles of Bull Run

The sound of the drums helped communicate commands to an entire army.

The First Battle of Bull Run was fought on July 21, 1861, near Manassas, Virginia. The battle, which the South called the Battle of Manassas, was the first major fight in the Civil War. General Irvin McDowell's Union Army fought a five-hour battle against 33,000 Confederates under Generals P.G.T. Beauregard and Joseph Johnston. At first, the Confederate Army retreated, but one division under-Colonel Thomas Jackson held out until General Johnston brought 9,000 reinforcements and forced the Union soldiers to retreat. Jackson's exceptional leadership meant he was promoted to major general. He was also given the nickname "Stonewall" for the way he stopped the Union Army like a wall.

The Second Battle of Bull Run was fought on August 28–30, 1862. It was also a great victory for the South. It was the decisive battle in the Confederates' Northern Virginia campaign and a major blow to the Union Army's hopes for a quick victory and a speedy end to the war.

A DECISIVE BATTLE

The Second Battle of Bull Run dashed Southern hopes that the North would let them peacefully separate, and Northern hopes that a show of force would convince the South to come back into the Union. Each side now understood that they were engaged in a long and bloody battle to resolve the fate of the United States.

★ Manassas, Virginia

Drummer Boys in the Civil War

Drummer boys, some as young as nine or ten years old, played a significant role in the war. Over 100,000 boys aged 15 and younger enlisted. Many of these boys ran away from home; others joined with their parents' consent. These boys not only led the troops into battle, but also served as orderlies for commanding officers and helped care for the wounded. They were often the first casualties, as they marched ahead of the troops.

Johnny Clem was a famous drummer boy who quit school at the age of ten and was adopted by the 22nd Massachusetts Regiment. They gave him a uniform in his size and a shortened rifle. Two years later he was allowed to join the Union Army. He was captured by a Confederate unit and later exchanged for a Confederate prisoner. He stayed in the army as a mounted orderly until he was discharged in 1864. After the war, President Grant appointed him second lieutenant in the army, where he served until 1915, retiring as a brigadier general.

General Thomas "Stonewall" Jackson

NO MORE MASTERS

Berea, Kentucky, 1867

MORNING... *"Cora, what you doin' dawdlin' like a caterpillar in the sun? Fetch my horse 'afore I lay the whip on you! Or sell you off like I sold your brother and sister. Cora!"*

"Cora?" Mr. Cunningham tapped his cane against Cora's desk. "Please join us!"

Cora's head snapped up. The dream was over. The whole class was staring at her. "Yes sir, Master Cunningham.

"I am not your *master*," Mr. Cunningham corrected her. "You are no longer a slave, Cora. Think like a free woman; talk like a free woman." His voice turned gentle. "You will learn, child; you will learn. Keep studying and work hard and one day you might be sitting in my chair."

"I could never do that, Mast…err, Mr. Cunningham." Cora met her teacher's gaze. "I am not smart enough. And besides, I am a girl."

"Being a girl makes no difference. You were smart enough to get into the school and smart enough to pass my mathematics class last term. That is a good head on your shoulders, Cora. You just need to use it. And that," Mr. Cunningham said with a smile, "means not thinking like a slave!"

Not think like a slave? How else can I think? I do not know another way to think.

Cora blinked. Her classmates were staring at her. *Here I go again, spinning spiderwebs, as Ma would say.* She looked up at her teacher. "I will try, sir."

A light April rain was falling as Cora left her classroom and walked onto the school grounds. She turned up the collar of her jacket. Mr. Cunningham wanted her to think like a free person, yet all her life she had been told what to do and when to do it. Her owner, Master Cockburn, had been firm with his slaves. *"Do what I tell you and there won't be no trouble…"*

No, Cora and her family had not known freedom. Even after she and Ma ran away to join the colored folks trailing after General Sherman's Union Army as it marched through Georgia, Cora had still done as she was told.

Northern soldiers, it turned out, didn't treat them much better than the slave owners. *Mr. Lincoln may have freed us*, she thought, *but most of Sherman's soldiers only saw the color of our skin.* She and Ma had struggled along with the army, but when Cora begged to return to the relative safety of Cockburn's plantation, Ma refused.

"What we goin' back to?" Ma would say when Cora complained of the damp and cold and lack of food. "You think Master Cockburn's gonna welcome us home? 'Hey you, Clara, Cora. Come into the big house and sit a spell. You're free folks now just like us.' You think he gonna say that?"

So on they'd gone, two women in a river of thousands of souls, rolling through Georgia searching for the Promised Land, where they'd be reborn. Cora and her mother didn't know it then, but that Promised Land was waiting for them in Kentucky. It was called Berea, and it took them three years to get there.

"Hey, Cora. I guess my dad is being hard with you again."

Cora turned to greet her friend Robert Cunningham. "He sure is. Tell me, Robert, how can you understand what we went through as slaves? Someone *owned* me." She grabbed his coat sleeve. "Like you own this coat. They *sold* my brother and sister. Can you imagine someone selling your sister and you never seeing her again?"

"I guess I can't." Robert looked embarrassed. "But you are free now, and your folks are counting on you. I remember the day your ma and pa brought you here. You had a cow tied to your wagon."

Cora's scowl turned to a smile. "That cow was my tuition for the school. It's still grazing in the field. I milk it as part of my school chores."

"Where'd your pa get that cow anyway?"

"He chopped wood for a white lady whose husband was killed in the war. She gave him the cow as payment. It was so scrawny, we thought it would die, but Ma cared for it and it fattened up pretty fast."

At that moment her friend Marylee joined them. Marylee had been a free black living in Kentucky before the war. Her parents owned a small farm about five miles from the school. They had sent her to Berea for an education.

"You talking about that cow again?" Marylee laughed and draped an arm over Cora's shoulder.

Robert poked Cora gently in the ribs. "Your folks worked hard for that cow. Don't disappoint them." The school bell rang. "We have to go back inside." He gave her an encouraging smile.

"Are you going to the wagon party on Saturday?" Marylee asked as they walked into the school.

Cora brightened. "I wouldn't miss it." Wagon parties were her favorite activity. Boys and girls, black and white, accompanied by teachers, rode in wagons up to the hills surrounding Berea, where they hiked and then enjoyed a picnic lunch.

As Cora sat at her desk, she looked around the room. True, she was the oldest student in the class, but it was a comfort to be mixed in with boys and girls, black and white. In Georgia, it had been a crime to teach a black person to read and write.

Not think like a slave? How else can I think? I do not know another way to think.

58

In Berea, it was considered an act of pride. Again, Cora thought what a miracle this place was, and what a great man Mr. Fee was for founding it. And yet, she still could not shake off the feeling of being less important than the white students.

It was a feeling as much a part of her as the color of her skin.

AFTERNOON... After school let out, Cora walked the short distance to her family's home on Center Street. The street had been designed as a place where black and white families would live together, thereby becoming friends, as well as neighbors. Cora and her parents had come to Berea from a Union Army camp in Kentucky—Camp Nelson, where 10,000 slaves were given freedom in exchange for serving in the Union Army. After the war, ex-slaves,like Cora and her mother had flocked to Camp Nelson to get their emancipation papers. To their delight, they were reunited with Cora's father, Reuben, who had run away at the start of the war to join the Union Army. It was at Camp Nelson, the place the blacks called their "cradle of freedom," that they heard about Berea.

"Hello, Ma," Cora called out as she entered the main room of their house.

"Cora." Her mother looked up from her sewing. She was a talented seamstress who made shirts and pants and dresses for many of the town's residents. Usually she was ready with coffee and fresh biscuits when Cora came home from school. Today, however, the air smelled of sweat, rather than fresh baking.

"Ma, what's wrong?" Cora crossed to where her mother sat in front of the fireplace. Her dark hair was covered with a bright red scarf and her usually happy eyes glittered with anger. "What's wrong, Ma?" Cora repeated.

"It's these trousers I'm makin' for Mr. Fee," she said. "He needs them tonight, but the buttons for the fly fell in the fire just as I was fixin' to sew them on."

"Fell in the fire? How'd that happen?"

"It's that cat." Her mother pointed to a ginger cat curled on the hearth. "That beast you call Savannah knocked the basket clean off my lap."

Cora tried not to laugh. "Ma, you know I'm not getting rid of Savannah. She's been with us ever since we crossed the Savannah River. Fished her out of the water, I did."

"Shoulda let her drown!" Clara clucked her tongue.

"Ma, if it's only buttons you're missing, I'll get them from Mr. Townsend's store."

"Thank you, Daughter." Her mother handed her a coin from her apron pocket.

Cora walked along Center Street to Middletown, where Mr. Charles H. Blythe and his brother owned several businesses, including a grocery store. Next door was Mr. Townsend's dry goods store. Cora shoved her hands into her pockets, lowered her head, and entered.

"Hey there, Cora," Mr. Townsend said.

"Afternoon, Mr. Townsend."

"And what can I do for you today?"

"Mama needs four buttons to finish Mr. Fee's pants."

Mr. Townsend pulled a box off the shelf behind him and set it on the counter. "Which buttons do you want?"

Cora examined the box and selected her favorite. "These. They're beautiful. Look at the brown swirls."

"They're made from a deer horn." Mr. Townsend wrapped the buttons in a square of brown paper and handed them back to her. "Is that all today, Cora?"

"Yes." Cora gave him her money.

Mr. Townsend dropped the coin into a box and handed Cora three pennies change. She slipped her change and the buttons into the pocket of her dress. "Mr. Townsend, can I ask you a question?"

"Of course." Mr. Townsend leaned across the counter.

"Have you always lived in Berea?"

"No. I grew up on a farm about fifty miles from here."

"Did your family own slaves?"

"No, but some of our neighbors did." He thought for a moment. "My folks hated slavery. They believed it was a great evil, and I agreed with them. When the war broke out, I joined the Union Army. After the war, I heard about Berea. I believe, as Mr. Fee does, that all people are equal and we should learn to live together." He peered at Cora from under bushy eyebrows. "Does that answer your question?"

Cora thought for a moment. "Sort of."

"What is still bothering you?"

"When Ma and I were traveling with the Union Army, lots of white folks ordered us around like we were still slaves."

"It is a sad fact, Cora, that not all people think alike. But remember that enough folks thought like I did to end slavery. It may not be ideal yet, but it is a start."

It is a start. Mr. Townswend had answered her question, but not her worry. Suddenly she noticed a commotion in the town square across the street. She walked over to the square and stopped in her tracks.

Cora stared in amazement. Before her was the tallest man she had ever seen. He stood straight as a tree trunk, lean, with shiny black skin and black eyes that seemed to look through a person. He was dressed in a black suit, stiff white shirt, and black string tie. A crowd had gathered around him. Mesmerized, Cora moved forward. "Brothers and sisters," the man's voice rang out, "I have come to bring you a message of freedom."

Cora moved closer. She recognized this man as one of the traveling preachers who went from town to town. There was an air of confidence about him that touched his audience. Simply watching him, Cora felt taller, stronger, and in control.

The man introduced himself as the Reverend Abraham Lincoln Warner. "I have taken the name of the great man who freed us," he said. "My message is simple: God loves all his children, black and white. And you, the people of Berea, are doubly blessed because John G. Fee believes that education will make you truly free."

When he was finished a young woman passed around a hat for contributions so the reverend could continue his good work. Cora lingered after the crowd dispersed. "Excuse me, Mr…"

"Abraham Lincoln Warner." The man held out his hand.

"What is your real name?"

The reverend laughed. "My slave name? I choose not to recall it. And what is your name, my good young woman?"

"Cora Brand."

"And how came you by that name?"

"My master named me."

"'Master.' That is a word I *never* want to hear again."

"That's what my teacher tells me when I call him 'master.'"

"And why do you call him that?"

Cora looked down.

"I cannot help myself."

"Look at me!"

Cora's head snapped up.

"Look me in the eye. You are a strong young woman and you are free. Why do you still think like a slave?"

"I was born a slave. My mother and my father were born slaves. My brother and sister were sold away from us."

"Stand up tall. You are a free woman with the spirit of God in your soul. Never forget that. You come to the church tonight. I will be speaking there with a very special lady. I think you need to hear what she has to say."

Cora stared after him as he marched off. *What a strange man,* she thought. But her curiosity was piqued.

"'Master.' That is a word I never want to hear again."

EVENING... The church was full when Cora arrived. She searched the crowd for a familiar face and then saw Marylee in the third row. She squeezed in beside her, causing a large woman on Marylee's right to complain loudly.

"I'm sorry, ma'am," Cora apologized.

"You young people! No manners," huffed the woman.

Cora and Marylee stifled giggles. "I didn't know you were coming," Marylee whispered.

"I met that man in the park." Cora pointed to Reverend Warner, who was sitting on stage next to a white woman. Something about her face struck a chord in Cora's mind. She was a handsome woman, with dark hair pulled off her face and fastened into a curl of braids at the nape of her neck. She wore a navy blue dress with a white collar and her lips curved into a soft smile as she surveyed her audience.

"Who is she?" Cora whispered to Marylee.

"That is Susan B. Anthony," responded the stout woman. She put a finger to her lips as the Reverend Warner stood and addressed the crowd.

"Ladies and gentlemen, tonight I have the honor to introduce to you a woman who has spent her life working for freedom and equal rights. She fought to abolish slavery, and today she comes to speak to us about another battle—equal rights for women in the United States of America. For her efforts she has been arrested for voting illegally, a notion at which she scoffs. Please welcome Miss Susan B. Anthony."

Miss Anthony stood, and the crowd broke into applause. She began to speak.

"Friends and fellow citizens, I stand before you tonight under indictment for the alleged crime of having voted at the last presidential election without having a lawful right to vote. It shall be my work this evening to prove to you that in thus voting, I not only committed no crime, but simply exercised my rights, guaranteed to me and all United States citizens by the national Constitution, beyond the power of any state to deny." She looked out at the audience and smiled. "I see here a mix of faces, black and white, sitting together as equals. It is a freedom that was hard won. But we won it!"

Again the audience roared. Cora clapped

61

so hard her hands hurt. Marylee had tears streaming down her cheeks.

"Now I have turned my efforts to achieving the vote for women. The dictionary defines a citizen as a person in the United States, entitled to vote and hold office. The only question left to be settled now is: Are women persons? And I hardly believe any of our opponents will have the hardihood to say they are not. Hence, every discrimination against women in the constitutions and laws of several states is today null and void, precisely as is every one against Negroes."

The audience went crazy. People clapped and cheered, and a few even stomped their feet. Cora felt as if she had suddenly come alive. Here was a white woman who had fought for the abolition of slavery and was now asserting her rights as a woman.

Cora, Marylee, and several of their schoolmates were standing outside the church. Cora looked up as the Reverend Warner approached.

"Well, young lady, I am glad to see that you came to the lecture."

"Yes." Cora greeted the Reverend Warner. "Thank you."

"So what did you think of Miss Anthony?"

Cora craned her neck so she could look into the the reverend's eyes. "I think she is wonderful."

"I do, too," said Marylee. "She fights for what she believes to be right and fair."

"But most of all, she believes in herself,"

"I see here a mix of faces, black and white, sitting together as equals. It is a freedom that was hard won. But we won it!"

said Cora excitedly.

"And now what did that teach you?" asked the reverend.

Cora shot him a questioning look. "To believe in myself?"

"As should we all," he replied. "Good night." He turned, tipped his hat, and walked back toward the church.

"What an interesting man," said Marylee.

Robert joined them. "My father says he goes from town to town, and people come from all over to hear him. So, Cora," he said, changing the subject, "are you going on the wagon party this Saturday?"

"Of course." Cora smiled. "I would not miss it. But now I had better get home or Ma and Pa will wonder where I've got off to."

They said good night, and as Cora walked to Center Street she thought about Miss Anthony's message. *Yes, women are strong.* Hadn't she and Ma survived with Sherman's army, made it to Camp Nelson, and found Pa? Cora lifted her head and looked at the sky. The moon was half full and surrounded by a thousand points of light. She recognized the drinking gourd and followed it to the North Star—the star that had guided them north to freedom.

"We found our cradle of freedom," she said to the star. *I think I understand now. Berea is like a bird's nest, housing and protecting us from the outside world. Yet nests are also places where baby birds learn how to live and then fly away to teach what they have learned.*

Cora went into the house. Her mother was in her rocking chair before the hearth, wrapped in a cocoon of firelight; Savannah lay curled in a ball at her feet. Her father sat at the table, reading the Bible by the light of a candle. Cora felt a glow of pride. As she learned to read, she was teaching Pa.

"Did you have a nice evening?" Ma asked her.

"Oh, yes." Cora sat on the floor beside her mother's chair. Savannah opened an eye, and Cora scratched her behind the ears. "I heard the most incredible woman speak," she said in a dreamy voice. "Her name is Susan B. Anthony. She helped free the slaves, Ma, and now she's fighting to get women the vote."

"Women to vote?" Pa looked up.

"Why not?" said Ma. "Women are people, too."

"That is what Miss Anthony said." Cora continued, "She said that women are people, just like men."

"Not exactly like men." Pa closed the Bible and stood. "Thank goodness for that. Right, Mama?" He put his arms around her and rested his chin on her head.

"Don't go gettin' mushy on me," Mama laughed. She wriggled free and turned to face them. "First we got freed, now Cora's goin' to school, and next we women will vote. What miracles will we see next?"

"We don't have the vote yet," said Cora.

"Honey, you keep studying and one day you can help Miss Anthony get it for us."

"But, Mama, how can I? I'm black!"

"I thought Miss Anthony said that all people are equal. That means black folks, too, doesn't it?"

Cora looked at her parents. Their faces were wreathed in smiles. They were proud of her. *And I'm proud of me, too,* thought Cora. *I am proud of all of us.* "Mama, Papa, I am glad we came to Berea. Black folks in other places don't have it this good, do they?"

"No," said her. father. "In lots of places even white girls don't get the kind of education you are gettin' here. Maybe someday more folks will think like Mr. Fee and Miss Anthony. Maybe you will be one of the people who lead the way."

Cora looked down at her hands. They were black but they were built the same as white folks' hands, fit for doing anything she wanted to do. *And so is my brain,* she thought. *The slave owners tried to make us feel stupid, but we know that is not true.* "I am as good as anyone else."

"What did you say?" asked her mother.

Cora looked up in surprise. She hadn't realized she was thinking aloud. "I said I am as good as anyone else."

"Of course you are," said her father. "What took you so long to figure that out?"

"I guess I've known it all along," said Cora. "I just had to get myself to believe it. And now I do." The test, she knew, would be to continue to believe in herself in the difficult world outside of Berea. Her challenge, then, was to work hard and build the strength she would need to face that situation when the time came. ✪

NO MORE MASTERS

Berea College

Berea College

Interracial schools were extremely rare at this time in the United States.

Berea College was founded in 1853 by John G. Fee, an abolitionist who had founded an anti-slavery church in the town of Berea. Fee spent the Civil War years at Camp Nelson in Kentucky, where he preached to and taught thousands of slave men who volunteered for the Union Army. When the war ended, he returned to Berea to build an interracial college and community. He invited African American families from Camp Nelson to settle in Berea, where they could get an education and begin new lives.

Berea College was the first institution of its kind in the United States. It was interracial and coeducational. By 1870, there were seven departments: Primary, Intermediate, Academy (high school), Preparatory, Normal, Ladies, and College. Girls and boys, black and white, studied reading, writing, arithmetic, the Bible, and English composition. The teachers were socially liberal men and women. Most came from Oberlin College in Ohio, and all were dedicated to Berea's ideals and strong moral code.

Berea College grew, moving to a larger building to accommodate more students.

John G. Fee

A Thriving Community

Fee planned the town of Berea to be integrated. Center Street was built as an interracial neighborhood where blacks and whites lived together. The business center was Middletown, where Mr. Charles H. Blythe and his brother owned several businesses, including a grocery store. An active social life developed, with literary societies, music programs, and traveling speakers who visited the town. Students of the college from outside the town either boarded with people in town or lived in dorms. They all did chores such as working in the kitchen, doing the laundry, and taking care of the grounds. There were daily prayer meetings, and students were required to attend church and Sunday school.

Berea, Kentucky

A PLACE IN HISTORY

SETTING AN EXAMPLE

Since it's founding, the college has been a model for interracial education. It is also seen as a challenge to other institutions. Berea was a leader in the fight for women's rights. Female students were encouraged to study non-traditional subjects, such as the classics and languages, that were generally reserved for men. Berea was a unique community where skin color, class, and gender did not matter. What did matter were work ethics, determination, and a willingness to work together. Berea set an example for other schools and communities—it continues to stand as a beacon of tolerance to this day.

THE LAST RAIL

Promontory Summit, Utah, 1869

MORNING... "Chan, our great adventure is almost finished." Chan's brother Huan grasped his shoulder. "Soon we can go home to China."

Chan squirmed. At 14, he was one of the youngest workers building the new transcontinental railroad. He had come here with Huan two years ago, and they sent most of the $28 a month they each made home to help their widowed mother raise their three brothers and two sisters. Huan was like his father—taking care of him on the long sea journey and since they had arrived in California. When the brothers signed on, the men who recruited Chinese workers said that Chan was too young for the job. But Chan was tall for his age and strong, so when Huan promised to care for him, the recruiters made an exception and hired him.

The brothers had planned to return to China once the job was over. But now, Chan wasn't so sure. He shivered. The sun had not yet risen and the predawn air was chilly. All around him workers stood waiting for the foreman to signal the start of the day's work.

A sudden quiet swept over the camp. Chan looked up as Benjamin Parsons, a construction supervisor for the Central Pacific Railroad, left his house—a building built on the flatcar of a train. Mr. Parsons came to stand in front of the assembled workers. His head was uncovered, exposing a fringe of white hair. A white beard sprouted under his lip and rested on the collar of his starched shirt. He looked at the crowd.

"Gentlemen, we are near the end of a monumental task. We have done what many thought to be impossible. Starting in Sacramento, California, we have cut a path through mountains rising up to 7,000 feet. We have blasted tunnels through cliffs of sheer rock. All of you are to be commended for your courage and hard work. And today," he said with a pause, "we will prove to Mr. Charles Crocker, the boss of the Central Pacific Railroad, that we can realize his dream by accomplishing one more impossible feat: we will lay ten miles of track in one day!"

A cheer went up from the crowd. Everyone knew of Mr. Crocker's bet with Vice President Durant of the Union Pacific Railroad. Mr. Durant said that laying ten miles of track in one day was impossible. Mr. Crocker was determined to prove him wrong. The Union Pacific Railroad had started in Omaha, Nebraska, and moved west, while the Central Pacific Railroad had started in California and moved east. The two would connect in Promontory Summit, Utah, where California's governor, Leland Stanford, would hammer in the last spike. Competition had been fierce to see which team would lay track the fastest.

"How will he do this?" Chan asked Huan.

"Mr. Parsons is very smart," Huan said, tapping his forehead. "His workers have been hauling the railroad ties ahead by horse teams."

"They set out the ties on the graded roadbed," said a redheaded man beside them. "The ties will be in place when we arrive with the rails. My name is George Fitzpatrick. I am one of the eight Irish rail handlers who were chosen to lay the rails." He pointed to Chan. "Come with me. I can use a strong helper."

"I will see you when we have won Mr. Crocker's bet for him," Chan said to Huan.

"Think about China while you are working," his brother called after him. "When this is over, you must decide on what to do with the rest of your life."

His words sent a chill down Chan's spine. He did miss home. But he had also come to love this wild new land and its promises for a better future. Yet it was his duty as a younger brother to listen to Huan and do what Huan thought was best for their family.

He did miss home. But he had also come to love this wild new land and its promises for a better future.

Chan walked with Mr. Fitzpatrick to the tracks. A train of sixteen cars loaded with iron rails and other building materials had been pushed forward to the point where the first rails would be laid.

"Hey, Chan, catch." A worker tossed a metal bar at him. Chan snatched it from the air.

"I still don't understand why they call these 'fish plates,'" he said, examining it.

"Me neither, but I would not want to eat fish off them," laughed Mr. Fitzpatrick.

Fish plates were actually used to bolt the ends of two rails together—something Chan had done a lot of over the past few weeks. He looked at the calluses that had formed on his hands after endless hammering and lifting.

"Chan, come and help us," shouted a man who was punching stakes into the side of a car.

"Watch out or you'll get hit," Chan called back, as another worker rolled rails off the car and down the stakes to the ground.

Mr. Fitzpatrick pulled out his pocket watch. "The crew cleared sixteen cars in eight minutes. Amazing!" He snapped the watch shut.

Now it was Chan's turn to work. He and Mr. Fitzpatrick and five Chinese men climbed onto a small iron hand cart. The crew loaded sixteen rails, a keg of bolts, a keg of spikes, and a bundle of fish plates.

"Hold on tight," Mr. Fitzpatrick shouted. Riders on two horses attached to the cart flicked their whips and the horses bolted quickly forward.

Chan clung to one of the barrels as the cart raced along the tracks. When they reached the end, he jumped down and a new crew climbed on board. Chan watched as they broke open the kegs, cut the fastenings on the fish plates, and tossed them to workers waiting on the side.

"Now it is my turn," said Mr. Fitzpatrick. He joined the other Irish handles, four on each side of the track. Two men seized the forward end of the rail while the other two slipped it sideways so it rested on iron rollers. Mr. Fitzpatrick and a partner moved ahead, and when the other two men dropped the rail into place, they bolted it down.

"Okay, step back. Let's let the 'pioneers' to do their job," said Mr. Fitzpatrick, pointing to three workers who were using shovels and their bare hands to attach the railroad ties to a rope line. The line was measured from spikes laid down by the

original surveyors to make sure the tracks were straight.

Chan looked down the line of workers, from the pioneers to the tampers. It stretched an incredible two miles. As one section was completed, the material train moved to the next. Chinese men in conical straw hats moved among the workers, distributing tea and water from buckets that hung from poles suspended across their shoulders. By the time the sun was at high noon and the workers stopped for lunch, six miles of track had been laid.

AFTERNOON... "So, younger brother, how is the work going?"

Chan looked up from his bowl of rice as Huan sank to the ground beside him.

"It is going well. We will succeed and win Mr. Crocker's bet for him. Do you not agree?"

Huan laughed. "Mr. Crocker will be happy with the results of today's work. When this is over, we will take our money and return to China." He gave his brother a stern look.

Chan didn't answer.

"Chan?" Huan turned so they were facing each other. "You *will* come home to China with me."

"No!" Chan jumped to his feet. "I will go to San Francisco to live. I will find a wife and have a family. I want many children."

Huan stared at him. Was his younger brother really defying him? "And how will you support them? There are no more railroads to build."

Chan lowered his eyes. *I owe my loyalty to Huan and to my family. Yet I do not want to live my life in poverty in China. If I stay here,*

I can send money home. Am I not more help that way?

They were interrupted by a commotion coming from the camp. A fight had broken out between a Chinese worker and one of the Irish rail handlers. The brothers rushed over. A dark-haired man with pale skin and bulging muscles was shouting at a Chinese man. Reaching over, he pulled the Chinese man's pigtail. The Chinese man waved his fists, but his opponent head-butted him so he fell and landed on his behind.

"What is going on here?" Mr. Parsons marched over.

"It is time for you coolies to go back to China where you belong," shouted the white man.

"See," said Huan as they walked away from the scene. "The white people do not want us here. There is no work for Chinese after the railroad."

"Yes, but people will need places to live. I have learned many skills." Chan's voice quavered. Was Huan right? Chan had heard from other workers that Chinese were not welcome in San Francisco. Most of the men planned to return to China, but the few who wanted to stay worried that the local populace would try to keep them out. Now, however, was not the time for serious talk. There was still four miles of track to be laid, and the day was moving on. When the foreman blew his whistle to resume work, Chan jumped to his feet.

"Today I will help make history. Tomorrow I will worry about the future."

"Perhaps when the railroad is done the white people will appreciate what good workers we Chinese are," he said.

Huan shook his head. "Good for what, younger brother? Cleaning their houses?"

"I can send more money home if I stay." *Can I?* As Chan walked back to Mr. Fitzpatrick and their car, this question whirled around in his brain. *I will not think of it for now*, he decided as he clambered atop a keg of bolts.

"Are you ready to finish the job?" Mr. Fitzpatrick called out when they were all on board.

"Let's go!" the men shouted back.

As the rider cracked his whip and the horses jumped forward, Chan's heart jumped, too. *Today I will help make history*, he thought. *Then tomorrow I will worry about the future.*

As the day wore on, the work became more difficult. The west slope of the Promontory Mountains was steep with sharp curves, and Chan was sweating by the time they reached their next stop. He paused to catch his breath and wipe his face with a cloth. Then he lifted a rail and carried it to where the workers were hammering the rails into shape. Chan set it down on a block and lifted a hammer. *Wham!* Sparks flew into the air. *Wham!* He hit it so hard the sound almost hid the rumble from the top of the hill. Almost, but not quite.

Chan's head snapped up. He saw a dust cloud shrouding a huge boulder that was coming toward him. "Run!" he shouted.

The men scattered as the boulder rolled downhill. Chan ducked to one side, and then turned back as he saw one of the workers stumble and fall. The man's leg bent under him at an unnatural angle.

He tried to rise, fell back, and screamed. Everyone froze, their eyes turned to the boulder as it rumbled down the hill. Closer, closer it came to the trapped man. He shouted louder.

Isn't anyone going to help him? thought Chan.

"Please, help me!"

Chan darted onto the track. He lifted the man over his shoulder and jumped aside seconds before the boulder rumbled by. Setting the man on the ground, Chan sank down beside him.

"Are you all right?" shouted Mr. Fitzpatrick as he raced over to the two men.

"Yes." Chan gave him a shaky smile.

"He saved my life," said the other man.

"He did indeed." Mr. Fitzpatrick clapped a hand on Chan's shoulder. He knelt down beside the injured worker. "It looks like your leg is broken." He signaled two medics, who rushed over with a stretcher. Other workers were crowding around, pounding Chan's shoulder and calling him a hero.

Mr. Fitzpatrick stood. "Good job, Chan." He looked down at the injured worker. "The doctor will fix up your leg. For the rest of you," he turned to the crowd, "get back to work. We have a railroad to finish!"

Fortunately the boulder had not damaged the tracks, and for the rest of the afternoon, Chan and the men advanced about a mile an hour. Cars filled with rails and other supplies rolled up and down the new track. Once a section was complete, the next train moved to the end of the newly laid track and the workers unloaded materials for the next two miles. The air was filled with the sound of hammers on steel, men shouting instructions, and the neighing of horses as their riders urged them forward. Alongside this chaos, the telegraph layers moved, setting up the poles and laying the wires of the newly expanded telegraph service. And at the very back of the line came the boarding house train, with its wooden houses built on top of flatcars, where the officers lived.

"Mr. Fitzpatrick," Chan shouted over the racket, "how much farther do we have to go?"

Mr. Fitzpatrick shielded his eyes and looked ahead. "I believe we are almost at the end, young man. We are laying the final two miles of track."

Chan's heart pounded as he unloaded the hand cart. He saw Mr. Parsons moving through the crowd, his white beard wagging up and down like a flag as he talked to the workers, thanking them for their hard work. Suddenly he heard a loud *whoop* starting at the front and rolling back like the rumble of thunder. Chan turned to Mr. Fitzpatrick. "What is it? What is happening?"

"We have done it!" Mr. Fitzpatrick shouted, throwing his arms in the air. He snapped open the gold watch that dangled from a chain across his chest. "Seven o'clock. We have broken all

Chan's head snapped up. He saw a dust cloud shrouding a huge boulder that was coming toward him. "Run!" he shouted.

records for laying track. I do believe that Mr. Crocker has won his bet!"

EVENING... That evening the entire camp celebrated. "Ten miles of track in one day! This is a record that will never be challenged," said Mr. Fitzpatrick. "Never again will there be such a spirited race to build a railroad. The competition between the Union Pacific and the Central Pacific railroads has spurred all of you to achieve what everyone thought to be impossible."

"So, younger brother, how do you feel now?" Huan said as they walked back to their tent.

"I am proud to be part of such a magnificent effort." Chan grinned. "But we are not yet finished."

"Yes, we must still lay the final miles of track." Mr. Fitzpatrick stood over them. He held out his hand. "You did a terrific job today, Chan. I am proud to work with you."

Chan felt warm with pleasure. Mr. Fitzpatrick started to leave and then stopped. "Chan," he turned back and studied the young man. "What are your plans?"

Chan and Huan exchanged pained looks.

"Chan will come with me back to China, where he belongs."

"Is that what you want, Chan?"

Chan hesitated.

"Is that what you want?" Mr. Fitzpatrick repeated, looking Chan in the eye.

"I do not know." Chan took a deep breath. "One part of my heart says, 'Go home. Your mother needs you.'"

"And the other part of your heart? What does it say?"

"'Stay here to help build this new land.'"

"A new land where Chinese are hated!" Huan spit in the dirt.

"We have been treated well by the railroad owners," said Chan.

"That is because they need us now. When the railroad is finished, they will want us to leave."

"I do not believe that," Mr. Fitzpatrick said. "I am Irish. We have had our share of problems settling in America, but look at me. I am making a life here."

"You are white!" Huan hissed. "We are Chinese! Besides," he looked at Chan, "I am the elder brother, and Chan will do what I say."

The two men glared at each other. Chan stepped between them. "This is a night of celebration. Let us not fight."

"We are not fighting," Mr. Fitzpatrick said quietly. "We are disagreeing." He turned on his heel to leave, then stopped and turned back. "Chan, I almost forgot what I came to tell you. Mr. Parsons wants you to be part of the eight-man Chinese crew that will lay the last section of rail. It is a tribute to your hard work and the dedication of all the Chinese workers who have helped to build this railroad."

After Mr. Fitzpatrick left, Huan and Chan retired into their tent. The night air was crisp and the brothers wrapped themselves in blankets against the chill. Soon Huan was sound asleep. Chan lay on his bedroll listening to his brother's snores. He closed his eyes, but sleep was far away. His mind was churning with the events of the day. Over and over he relived his rescue of the trapped worker and then, later, the triumphant moment when the railroad crew realized they had done the impossible. The shouts, the cries, the sheer exultation rang in his ears and danced before his eyes.

Careful not to wake his brother, Chan crept from the tent. Outside, he stood and stretched. Most people were asleep after the long, arduous day. A few sat around fires, drinking tea and talking. Chan did not want to talk. He needed to think. He walked away from the camp toward the railroad. When he reached it, he sat on the embankment and looked down at the tracks, gleaming in the moonlight like silver ribbons. He looked up at the sky, a giant black bowl studded with points of light. The night was clear with a full moon. *The same moon that shines on China*, he thought. Yet life there was so different. His family were peasants. They would always be peasants. Their job was to work on the land. Sometimes there was enough to eat; at other times the rains drowned the crops and people starved. The money that he and Huan sent home helped their mother feed their family. If he went back to China, where would the extra money come from? And even more important for Chan, if he went back to China, how would he ever get off the land?

"In America, even if they do not like

> **"In America, even if they do not like the color of my skin or the shape of my eyes, I can use my hands and my skills to make a life."**

the color of my skin or the shape of my eyes, I can use my hands and my skills to make a life." But would he find work once the railroad was done? He knew that white laborers blamed the Chinese for stealing their jobs. There had been demonstrations with Chinese workers injured. Many returned to China while others stayed, living in fear of the white workers' revenge.

Yet what was there for him in China? Chan pictured the family home, a one-room shack where seven people lived. *When I came here, I was a child. Since then, I have become a man. Huan thinks it is his duty to tell me what to do. But I want to guide my own life. Yet Huan is family, and to a Chinese person, family comes first.*

Chan buried his head in his hands. He held his breath and waited for his heart to speak, but his heart was silent. He waited for his head to tell him what to do, but his head was silent. After a moment he stood. *I do not have to decide today. I will finish my job on the railroad and then make my decision.*

Chan's step was heavy as he walked back to the camp. Yet as he got closer, it lightened. And by the time he reached his tent, he knew what his decision would be. ✪

★ ★ ★ ★ ★

THE LAST RAIL
The First Transcontinental Railroad

On May 10, 1869, Governor Leland Stanford drove the Golden Spike (also called the Last Spike) which symbolized completion of the country's first transcontinental railroad. It linked the east coast with California, opening up the American West. The Pacific Railway Act of 1862 had chartered two private companies. The Union Pacific Railroad started in Omaha, Nebraska, and built a line heading west. Meanwhile, the Central Pacific started in Sacramento, California, and built a line going east. The two lines met at Promontory Summit, Utah, where the ceremony for the Last Spike in the railroad was performed.

The railroad's route followed the Oregon, Mormon, and California trails—the wagon pathways used by settlers moving west. The rail line followed the Platte River, cut through the Rocky Mountains, crossed the desert in Utah and Nevada, and then went over the Sierra Nevada Mountains to Sacramento, California.

The tracks that were laid often stretched in a straight line as far as the eye could see.

Chinese Workers

Thousands of Chinese laborers were brought from China to work on the railroad. They performed difficult and dangerous tasks, using techniques they had learned in China, such as being lowered down cliffs in baskets to chip away at rock. The men were paid in cash at the end of each month, although the Chinese were paid less than white workers. Many sent their wages home to help support their families back in China. The Chinese laborers are credited with enabling the railroads to be built on time and built well.

Promontory
Summit, Utah

Chinese laborers
had to deal with
lower wages and
discrimination
when they came
to America.

The railroad changed
how people traveled
across the country.

The World's First Mass Media Event

When Governor Stanford hammered the ceremonial Golden Spike into place, it was probably the world's first live-media event. The hammers and the spike were wired to the telegraph line so that each hammer blow was transmitted as a click to telegraph stations all over the country and heard nationwide.

A PLACE IN HISTORY

OPENING UP THE WEST

Before the railroad was completed, moving west was difficult and dangerous. People traveled in covered wagons and on horseback. They had to cross rivers, climb over mountains, and ride through deserts where there was no water. The railroad reduced the trip from several months to a few days. At first, the transcontinental railroad only connected Omaha to Sacramento. In August 1870, the Kansas Pacific line was connected to the Denver Pacific line, completing the first real Atlantic-to-Pacific railroad. On June 4, 1876, an express train traveled from New York to San Francisco in a record 83 hours and 39 minutes!

FINDING SARAH

Johnstown, Pennsylvania, 1889

MORNING... At first, Anna didn't know where she was. And then she remembered. The flood! The disaster had destroyed her house, her town, and life as she knew it. For a moment, she lay on the cot staring at the canvas walls. *My temporary home*, she told herself.

Already, survivors of the Johnstown Flood were clearing debris and starting to rebuild. Her father had pitched this tent on a site near their ruined house. The Watson family was lucky. She, her sister, brother, and both parents were alive. So many others were dead or missing. Anna blinked back tears. Their neighbor, Mr. Carmichael, tried to save his five-year-old daughter, Sarah, who had fallen into the raging waters. Mr. Carmichael drowned. Sarah was one of hundreds of people who were still missing.

"Anna, good morning." Her mother poked her head through the tent flap. "There is good news."

Good news? How could anything be good amidst the horror of their situation?

"Clara Barton has arrived," her mother continued.

"Who is Clara Barton?"

"She nursed soldiers during the Civil War and founded the American Red Cross. She has brought other nurses with her, and they are going to help us tend to the wounded."

Anna stood and stretched. Her back ached and her muscles were cramped. The other cots in the tent were empty.

"Where is Benny?"

"Benny is working with the men in the valley."

Anna nodded. All the men were helping to clear the flood debris, and at 17, Benny was strong enough to help. "What about Mary?" She looked for her young sister.

"I took Mary to visit Mrs. Carmichael. It cheers her to have the child around, and it leaves you free to work in the hospital."

Each time Anna stepped out of the tent she was newly

amazed by the force of the flood's devastation. Even five days later, the devastation was overwhelming. The first morning after the flood, survivors had awoken to an eerie silence. The water had receded, leaving piles of mud and big chunks of debris. Whole city blocks were demolished. Remnants of clothing, bits of crockery, and pieces of furniture studded the debris. Hundreds of people were buried in the rubble. Rescuers were frantically searching for survivors.

Once again Anna relived the terrifying moment when her father had raced into the house calling to everyone to climb to the attic.

"The dam broke," he shouted. "The dam broke!"

Anna looked out the window and saw a wall of water, mud, and debris roaring toward them.

"Get up as high up as you can," her father ordered.

Anna followed her family as they scrambled up a ladder into the attic loft. They huddled together as the roar of the flood engulfed them. The noise was deafening—as if the entire world were crashing over their heads. The house shook so hard Anna was certain it would collapse. Beneath them, the water rose and rose, until only by standing on tiptoe was Anna able to keep her head above the muck. Her father lifted Mary until her head touched the roof. No one spoke; they could barely breathe. Anna

The first morning after the flood, survivors had awoken to an eerie silence. The water had receded, leaving piles of mud and big chunks of debris. Whole city blocks were demolished.

peeked through the attic window and saw a roof float by with people clinging to its surface. A wet, muddy mattress with a child on top tumbled past. A man on the roof was stretched out trying to reach her.

"Anna." Her mother's touch brought her back to the present. "Are you all right?"

"I was remembering the flood," Anna said with a shudder.

"I know. It is hard to forget. But we must be brave and help the survivors."

"Yes, Mama." Anna squeezed her mother's hand. "I will try."

AFTERNOON... The city's only hospital was a private institution on Prospect Hill that belonged to the Cambria Iron Company. The Philadelphia Red Cross had rushed to help. Doctors from the cities of Altoona and Philadelphia had come to Johnstown to treat survivors, but the hospital was soon filled to overflowing. On June 1, the city had set up a second hospital on Bedford Street, and that too was crammed with the sick and wounded. Anna was amazed at the amount of food, medicine, and supplies that were arriving in Johnstown every day from good people who were horrified at the disaster. And now Clara Barton had come to help. Anna knew all about the Angel of the Battlefield who had founded the American Red Cross to nurse wounded soldiers during the Civil War.

Anna threaded her way through piles of debris. In the center of town she saw a group of tents where the hospital was rising out of the mud. She recognized the doctor's wife, Mrs. Peabody, talking to a dark-haired woman in a blue dress covered by a long white apron. A brooch with a red cross on a white background was pinned to the throat of her bodice. Anna approached them.

"Excuse me, Mrs. Peabody. I've come to help."

"Bless you, Anna. We can use every able-bodied person. Anna, this is Clara Barton. She is organizing a hospital."

Anna took Miss Barton's hand. "We are very pleased to have you here. I want to be a nurse, just like you."

Clara Barton smiled. "This is a good place for you to start your training." She pointed to the tents. "These will be for the wounded. And those," she pointed to a second group of tents, "are 'hotels' for people who have lost their homes. Are you one of them?"

"No. Our home is filled with mud, but it is still standing. We're living in a tent now, but my father says he can fix the house." Anna turned to Mrs. Peabody. "Is there any word yet about Sarah Carmichael?"

Mrs. Peabody shook her head. "I'm afraid not. So many people are still missing. Every day that passes after the flood makes it less likely we will find more survivors."

Anna fought back tears. Even five days after the disaster, she refused to give up all hope.

Clara Barton had brought a staff of fifty doctors and nurses. Anna saw that they were all busy tending to the wounded and homeless. "What can I do to help?" She swung around as an agonized cry filled the air. Everyone stopped what they were doing as a woman, her clothes in ribbons, her hair caked with mud, staggered toward them. When she reached Anna, she held out her arms, then dropped to the ground.

Two nurses raced over with a stretcher. "I'll get the doctor." Miss Barton turned to Anna. "Stay with her. When she wakes up, she will want to see a friendly face."

Anna followed the stretcher and watched as the nurses carefully transferred the woman to a cot and covered her with a blanket. Anna pulled up a folding chair and sat by her side. A moment later, the woman's eyelids fluttered and she looked at Anna. Then she bolted into an upright position. "Where is she?" She looked wildly around.

"Where is who?"

"The girl who was with me under the bridge."

"The bridge! Were you at the bridge?"

Of all the horrors visited on Johnstown, the fire at the bridge had been the worst. A mountain of debris had washed down-river and pushed against the old stone railroad bridge. Telephone poles, trees, animals, machinery, and freight cars created an oil-soaked jam that trapped over five hundred people. Some were able to climb over the heap and reach safety on shore. Others were stranded, unable to free themselves from barbed wire and debris. And then the oil floating on the water

The house shook so hard Anna was certain it would collapse. Beneath them, the water rose and rose, until only by standing on tiptoe was Anna able to keep her head above the muck.

caught fire. Eighty people were killed and many others badly burned. And this woman had been there.

Anna looked at her. The woman's eyes were wide with fright, as if she was reliving the terror. Her face and arms were scratched, but there were no burn marks. A nurse brought a cup of water and put it to her lips. Anna took her hand. "Can you tell me what happened?"

The woman nodded. "I was on a mattress that washed up against the bridge. I was holding on to a little girl. She had blond curls and blue eyes. I held her tight so she wouldn't fall into the water. And then we were at the bridge and people were piling into us, and something big hit the mattress and she was gone!" She buried her face in her hands and sobbed.

At that moment Dr. Peabody came into the tent. He was a kindly man with gray hair and light blue eyes behind wire-rimmed spectacles.

"This woman was at the bridge," Anna said.

"That was five days ago." The doctor bent down so his face was level with the woman's. "Where have you been since?"

"I don't know."

"What is your name?"

"I think it is Rachel."

The doctor sighed. "The shock has erased much of her memory. Keep her warm and fed. Hopefully, it will return. I must go," he said in a sad voice. "There are so many people who are in much

"I was at the Cambria hospital. It is so overcrowded. Thank goodness the Red Cross is setting up hospital tents to take the overflow."

worse condition."

Anna sat next to Rachel and continued to hold her hand. The woman closed her eyes. Anna thought she was sleeping, but all at once Rachel spoke. "The girl was talking about someone called Sally." She closed her eyes again and this time fell asleep.

Anna stood and left the tent. There, she found Clara Barton standing outside.

"I was watching you," said Miss Barton. "You have a kind and caring nature. You will make a very good nurse."

Anna beamed. She promised to come back the next day.

EVENING... Anna arrived home the same time as her mother. "I was at the Cambria hospital," her mother said. "It is so overcrowded. Thank goodness the Red Cross is setting up hospital tents to take the overflow."

"I met Miss Barton." Anna smiled shyly. "She said that I am very caring and will make a good nurse."

"What a lovely compliment." Mrs. Watson put an arm around her daughter's shoulders. "Trials such as these are sent to test us and make us stronger."

"Why do the trials have to be so horrible?" Anna felt the tears welling up again. She blinked them back. "I sat with a woman who is in such shock that her memory is gone. She was at the bridge."

"Oh my!" Mrs. Martin shuddered. "She remembers nothing?"

"Only that she was on a mattress

clutching a child and then the child was gone. She doesn't even know where she's been these past five days."

"Mama, Mama, look what Mrs. Carmichael gave me." Mary bounced into the house. She was holding a porcelain doll. "Mrs. Carmichael says that her name is Sally."

Anna looked at the doll and gasped. "This is Sarah's doll. If Mrs. Carmichael is giving it away, she is also giving up hope."

Her mother shook her head. "It *has* been five days." She averted her gaze, but Anna knew that she was crying.

"Mama, we should make supper. Father and the boys will be home soon, and they will be very hungry."

Mrs. Watson wiped her eyes with the tip of her apron. "Yes," she sniffed. "At least there is food. People have been so generous sending supplies."

Benny had cleared a space in front of the house where the family could sit and eat. Mrs. Watson spread a blanket. Because it was June, it was still daylight when they sat down to their supper of bread, cheese, canned beans, and peaches.

"Once we are finished clearing the valley, we will rebuild the house," Mr. Watson said. "It's amazing how much has already been done. Within hours of the disaster, messages were telegraphed around the country and relief started pouring in. By two o'clock on Sunday, hospital equipment had arrived from Pittsburgh. And relief and money continues to arrive."

"Miss Barton says that newspapers all over the country have run stories about the disaster," said Anna.

"Imagine! Being able to send for help by wire and getting such immediate response," said her mother.

"Many of the men working with us in the valley have come from other towns." Benny took a piece of bread and cleaned out the last of the beans from his bowl. "There are people here from Philadelphia and as far away as Boston!"

Anna leaned back on her hands and looked up at the sky. The first stars were blinking in the gathering darkness. She looked at Mary, who was clutching Sarah's doll. With a jolt, she recalled Rachel's words in the hospital: "The girl was talking about someone called Sally."

"Mama," said Anna, "do you remember last year when Sarah wandered off to look for her lost doll?"

"I do. She had half of Johnstown searching for her. She scared us all to death."

"But we did find her. She was in the old schoolhouse…"

"Yes," said her mother. "On the hill above the railroad bridge…"

"Rachel said the child she was holding disappeared near the bridge."

"Before or after the fire?" asked their father.

"She doesn't remember."

Everyone jumped up.

"Benny and I will go and look," said Mr. Watson.

"I'm coming with you," Anna said.

"Oh my. Is it possible?" Mrs. Watson cupped her face in her hands. "I will go tell the Carmichaels."

Anna looked at the doll and gasped. "This is Sarah's doll. If Mrs. Carmichael is giving it away, she is also giving up hope."

"No!" said Mr. Watson. "Stay here until we come back. We can't give them any false hope."

Walking to the schoolhouse was treacherous, but Mr. Watson had found three lanterns that worked. Slowly, carefully, they made their way through the ruined town. The moon had risen by the time they saw the schoolhouse, a dark smudge on the crest of the hill. Holding the lantern high, Anna entered the building.

"Sarah," she called out. "Sarah, are you here?"

"Shhh." Benny put a finger to his lips. In the silence, they heard a soft moan.

"Over there." Mr. Watson pointed his lantern toward a corner of the room.

In the flickering light, Anna saw a shape covered in blue cloth. "Sarah!" She ran over to the girl, who was curled into a ball, her head on a pile of straw.

"Rachel?" The shape moved. "I'm so hungry. I finished all the apples. Where did you go?"

"Sarah!" Benny picked up the child.

"You're alive!" Anna couldn't believe her eyes.

"Where's Rachel?" Sarah blinked. "I know you. You're Anna."

"Yes, I'm Anna. And this is my father and my brother, Benny. And we've come to take you home."

It was after midnight when the exhausted family returned. Mrs. Watson ran to tell the Carmichaels, who raced over, unable to believe what they were seeing.

"Sarah!" Mrs. Carmichael sank to the ground rocking the girl in her arms.

"We found her sleeping in the old schoolhouse," said Mr. Watson. "She survived on apples. This woman, Rachel, whom Anna met in the hospital, must have carried Sarah up the embankment before the fire broke out. Sarah led her to the schoolhouse. The next morning Rachel said she was going for help and told Sarah to wait for her. But she never came back. Rachel has amnesia. She thinks she lost Sarah by the bridge."

"Maybe when I tell her we found Sarah, her memory will return," said Anna.

"She must have people looking for her, too," said Mrs. Watson. "I'm so proud of you, Anna."

"There are still so many people missing," said Mrs. Carmichael.

"We'll just have to keep looking," said Mr. Watson.

"Yes," said Anna. "One person at a time."

Anna sat outside the tent and looked up at the sky. It was clear, with no sign of the angry, rain-filled clouds that had caused the disaster. Already people were rebuilding. Clara Barton had promised to stay in Johnstown as long as she was needed. The scope of the tragedy was enormous, but so was the response from people all over the United States, and from other countries as well. Medicine and other supplies kept arriving. Doctors and nurses were working around the clock to help the injured. And a few people were

Tonight, perhaps, she would sleep without bad dreams, because now she had something to look forward to.

still being found alive. Sarah was safe. Tomorrow Mrs. Carmichael would take her to see Rachel, and hopefully Rachel's memory would return. Mrs. Carmichael had offered to watch Mary so Anna could continue to work in the hospital.

I'm going to be a nurse, thought Anna. *Clara Barton will train me, and I'll be part of the American Red Cross.* The thought made her proud. Tonight, perhaps, she would sleep without bad dreams, because now she had something to look forward to. ✪

FINDING SARAH
The Johnstown Flood

The American Red Cross built hotels like this one to house the homeless flood survivors.

At 4:07 in the afternoon, May 31, 1889, the people of Johnstown heard a roar like thunder as an enormous wave of water, debris, and mud descended on their town. The South Fork Dam, which had long been in need of repair, had broken under the strain of a violent rainstorm. An incredible twenty million tons (18 million metric tons) of water created a giant 36 foot (11 meter) wave that swept through the narrow valley in which Johnstown was built.

Swept Downstream

The people swept downstream were caught in a grinding mix of debris that included parts of buildings, vehicles, barbed wire, and furniture. Some clung to rooftops; others rode mattresses as if they were life rafts. Over two thousand people were killed and many others wounded. The worst part of the disaster occurred at the old railroad bridge, where oil from machinery and vehicles coated the water and eventually caught fire, killing eighty people and wounding many more.

This photo shows just how powerful the flood waters were.

Main Street, Johnstown, after the flood.

84

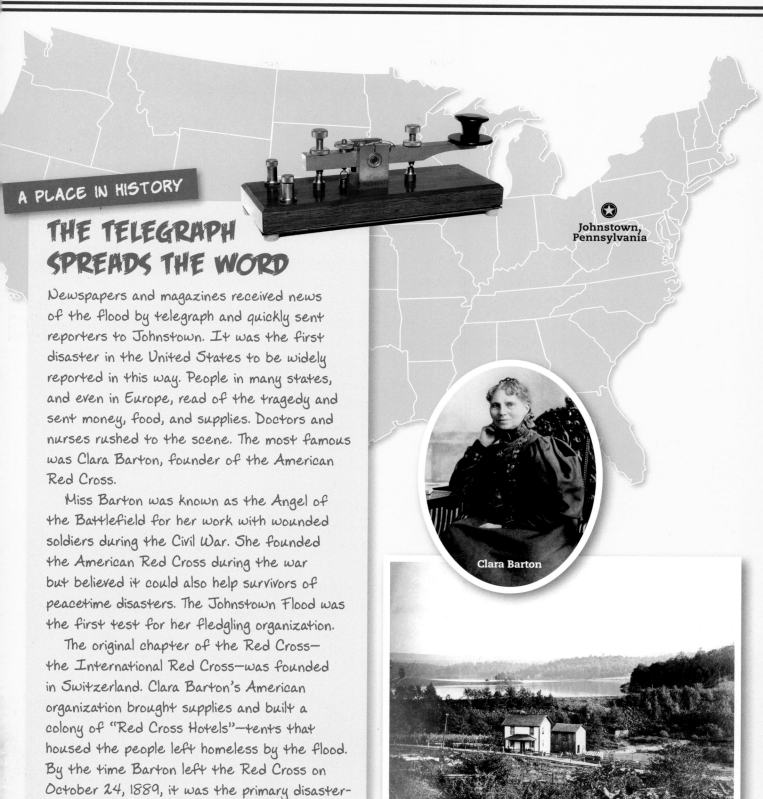

A PLACE IN HISTORY

Johnstown,
Pennsylvania

THE TELEGRAPH SPREADS THE WORD

Newspapers and magazines received news of the flood by telegraph and quickly sent reporters to Johnstown. It was the first disaster in the United States to be widely reported in this way. People in many states, and even in Europe, read of the tragedy and sent money, food, and supplies. Doctors and nurses rushed to the scene. The most famous was Clara Barton, founder of the American Red Cross.

Miss Barton was known as the Angel of the Battlefield for her work with wounded soldiers during the Civil War. She founded the American Red Cross during the war but believed it could also help survivors of peacetime disasters. The Johnstown Flood was the first test for her fledgling organization.

The original chapter of the Red Cross—the International Red Cross—was founded in Switzerland. Clara Barton's American organization brought supplies and built a colony of "Red Cross Hotels"—tents that housed the people left homeless by the flood. By the time Barton left the Red Cross on October 24, 1889, it was the primary disaster-relief organization in the U.S., and she was regarded as a hero.

Clara Barton

The picture shows Lake Conemaugh in the background. When the South Fork Dam broke, these were the waters that flooded Johnstown.

85

A NEW HOPE

Chicago, Illinois, 1899

MORNING... Rain drumming on the window woke Luisa. It was still dark, but she knew by the street sounds—the clip-clop of horse's hooves and the rattle of milk bottles—that dawn was near. Beside her, Sophia stirred. Luisa reached out and stroked her baby sister's fine hair, which was black, much like her own. At thirteen, Luisa was responsible for Sophia. It was a responsibility she took seriously, and lately Sophia worried her. She was pale and didn't smile or play. Luisa looked over to the bed her older sister, Rosa, and her mother shared in the corner of the room. It was empty. That meant they had left for their day's work in a dress factory.

Slipping from bed, Luisa shivered as her bare feet hit the cold floorboards. Her thin nightdress offered little protection from the chilly November air. She took a sweater from a peg near the door and slipped it on. Then she went into the small room that served as a kitchen and a living room. Luisa walked to the stove, took a match from the box nailed to the wall, and struck it against the side of the box. She held the match to the oven, jumping back at the *whoosh* of gas that escaped as a flower of blue flame blossomed around the burner. She held her hands over the fire and sighed as it warmed her frigid fingers. November was a cruel month in Chicago, and she longed for the sunshine of Naples, Italy, where she was born.

How will we survive the winter without Pa? she thought. Her father, Antonio Russo, had supported his family by working in the stockyards—that is, until he came home one night last spring burning with fever. Two weeks later he was gone, killed by the same typhoid fever as her brother, Carlo, the previous winter. Luisa's mother, Maria, had been struggling to feed her family ever since.

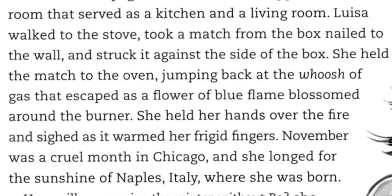

Luisa lifted the kettle from the stove and carried it to the sink. She ladled water from a bucket she had filled at the pump at the back of the house the previous day. She set the kettle on top of the stove. A wail from the bedroom made her jump. Sophia was awake and wanting her breakfast. But when Luisa went to her sister, she knew at once that something was wrong. Sophia's face was scrunched into a mask of pain; her legs were pulled up to her chest and her fists pounded the air.

"What is it? What is hurting you?" Luisa lifted the child and was terrified to feel the heat radiating from the small body. It was like picking up a hot coal. *Does Sophia have the fever, like Papa?* Luisa shivered. *No! You cannot be sick. You will not die! What can I do?* she thought. And then she remembered her neighbor Mrs. DeLuca telling her mother about Hull House, the settlement house started by Jane Addams.

"They help people in your situation," Mrs. DeLuca had said after Papa died.

"They give charity," Mama had responded. *"The Russos do not accept charity."* She folded her arms across her chest.

"At least look into what services they offer," said Mrs. DeLuca.

"Please, Mama," Luisa pleaded.

But to no avail. Maria Russo was staunchly opposed to charity of any kind. For her, accepting charity was almost as bad as stealing—that was that. But now, as Luisa looked at the crying baby in her arms, she made a decision. *Asking for help for a sick baby is not seeking charity.* "We are going to see Miss Addams," she said aloud to Sophia, holding her sister close to her chest. "I will not let you die because of false pride."

Luisa cradled Sophia under her coat, hoping her own body heat would protect the sick child. The rain had stopped, but the air remained damp and cold. As she walked through the garbage-strewn streets, she kept telling herself that she was doing the right thing. *Mama will thank me for getting Sophia well.* Her arms ached from carrying the child. She shifted her hold and Sophia whimpered. "Hush." She kissed the top of the child's head. She looked up and saw that she was in front of a stately brick building on Halstead Street. A sign said *Hull House.* Luisa paused, took a deep breath, and walked through the gate and up the steps.

When she entered Hull House, she stared in awe. She had never seen anything so grand. Unlike the dark and cramped rooms of her family's apartment, Hull House was spacious and airy. Her feet sank into the carpet that covered the front hall. To her left, a staircase rose straight and tall to the second floor. To her right was a large room with wooden chairs set around several low tables with lamps that cast a warm glow. She longed to sink into one of the chairs and never get up.

"Is she hungry?" A young woman stepped up to Luisa.

"She is sick. She has a fever."

The woman reached out to take the baby. Luisa handed her over and stretched her arms to relieve them from the strain

> **She knew at once that something was wrong. Sophia's face was scrunched into a mask of pain; her legs were pulled up to her chest and her fists pounded the air.**

of carrying Sophia. The woman gave her a sympathetic smile as she cradled Sophia in her arms. "She is so small."

"She's over one year old, but she *is* small," said Luisa.

The woman nodded. "First, let us take care of the fever. Then we can fill her with good food and fatten her up." She studied Luisa. "You could use some fattening as well."

Luisa was suddenly aware of how she must look to this elegant lady with her brown upswept hair, her starched white shirtwaist, and the gold watch that she wore on a chain around her neck. Luisa's clothes were plain and had been patched so many times that Luisa sometimes felt as if she were wearing a quilt.

The woman held out a hand. "I am Julia Lathrop. I am a resident here at Hull House. I help Miss Addams and Miss Starr. Please come with me." When Luisa hesitated, she took her arm. "What is your name?"

"Luisa. Luisa Russo."

"And the baby's name?"

"Sophia. She is my sister."

"And your mother? Where is she?"

"She works at the Johnstone Shirtwaist Factory. My sister, Rosa, works there, too."

"I see." Miss Lathrop's blue eyes darkened. She looked at Luisa. "So you take care of your sister."

Luisa nodded. She shuffled her feet. "I…I…my mother does not know I have come here," she said quickly. "She says that the Russos do not accept charity, but I don't

> "I…I…my mother does not know I have come here," she said quickly. "She says that the Russos do not accept charity, but I don't want my sister to die."

want my sister to die." She stared at her shoes, afraid to look Miss Lathrop in the eye. Then she lifted her head. "My papa and brother died of the typhoid fever…"

"And you are afraid that your sister has the same sickness." Miss Lathrop bent down and cupped Luisa's chin in her hand. "You did the right thing. Let's take Sophia to the infirmary. Our residents will know how to treat a sick child."

AFTERNOON… Once Sophia was settled in a crib in the nursery, Miss Lathrop took Luisa into the dining room. Seated at a long table with other children and some adults, she ate a bowl of thick vegetable soup, bread and butter, and a glass of milk that was set down before her. Luisa stared at the food in awe. Real butter and chunks of meat floating in the soup! *If we had food like this at home, Sophia would not be sick. Maybe Papa would not have died!*

When the meal was over, she returned to the nursery, where she found Sophia asleep. A handsome woman with lively brown eyes and dark brown hair pulled off her face was standing at the crib. She turned as Luisa approached. Luisa had seen Miss Addams's picture in newspapers and on posters and thought her pretty. In person she exuded a sense of strength and courage that reached out and enveloped Luisa like a warm cloak. Miss Addams looked from Luisa to the sleeping baby and then back.

"I do not believe your sister has typhoid," she said.

"*Grazie a Dio*." Luisa touched the gold cross she wore at her throat.

"She may have influenza, and that can be equally dangerous." At Luisa's outcry, Miss Addams held up her hand. "I am not a doctor, but I would like to have one see your sister. You can stay with us while we wait for Dr. Reynolds to come. He often visits our children."

"Do you mean have us stay the night?" Luisa swallowed hard.

Miss Addams gave her a kindly smile. "We have beds and," she said, taking in Luisa's bedraggled appearance, "a bathhouse for you to have a bath."

Luisa imagined sitting in a steaming tub of hot water and washing away the grime of the tenement, then slipping into a soft bed and sleeping through the night.

How nice it would be to accept Miss Addams's invitation. Luisa imagined sitting in a steaming tub of hot water and washing away the grime of the tenement, then slipping into a soft bed and sleeping through the night. She was about to tell Miss Addams yes when she remembered her mother and sister.

"My mother will be worried if I am not at home when she comes back from the factory. And she will want Sophia there as well."

Miss Addams thought for a moment. "You can leave Sophia with us while you go home. Then bring your mother and sister back to us. By then, Dr. Reynolds will have seen Sophia and we can talk about how to treat her."

Leave Sophia with strangers? Luisa felt as if she'd been asked to cut off her arm. Yet what Miss Addams said made sense. Why take a sick child back onto the cold, wet streets to an unheated flat? *Mama gave me the responsibility of caring for Sophia,* she thought. *I shall make the decision I feel is best.* She smiled at Miss Addams. "Thank you, ma'am. I will do that."

As she prepared to leave, Luisa turned to Miss Addams. "You and Miss Lathrop and all the women here are so kind. I would like…I would…" she stammered.

"What would you like?" Miss Addams gave her an encouraging smile.

"I want to go back to school so I can be like you," Luisa said. Then she turned and fled out the door.

As she walked home, Luisa's feet danced over the pavement. Hull House was all that she had envisioned and more. It was beautiful, and the people who ran it were kind and caring. Surely they would help Sophia. Before she left, Miss Addams had told her of the many classes and services the settlement house offered. *We have a coffee house for people to meet and socialize,* she had said.

That would be good for Mama, Luisa thought. Since her father's death, her mother had been quite lonely. Her only outings were to the factory and to church on Sunday.

It was raining again. Luisa pulled her coat tighter around her chest. She hunched her shoulders as she hurried through the crowded streets. When she reached the tenement, she dashed into the hallway, and her good mood disappeared like smoke in the rain. Luisa looked down at her arms, empty of the bundle they had earlier carried. And it hit her. She had left her sister in the care of strangers! Her mother was going to kill her.

EVENING... "You did *what?!*" Maria Russo was so angry that Luisa thought her head would explode. It took all Maria's control not to slap her daughter right across the face. "You took my baby to beg for charity and then you *left* her with strangers?!"

"Mama, I can explain."

"You had better," Rosa whispered.

Luisa whirled around. "You can be smart now, Rosa, but what would you have done? Next time, Mama can leave *you* to stay home and care for the baby."

"And *you* can sit in the factory in front of a sewing machine ten hours a day, until your fingers bleed and you think your back is going to snap in two."

"At least you get paid for your work," said Luisa.

"*Pennies.* That is what I get. And since when do you call caring for Sophia work? You always say how much you love her."

"Enough! Stop it, girls!" Mrs. Russo interrupted. "The important thing now is Sophia."

"Yes, Mama. And that is why I took her to the settlement house," explained Luisa. "Sophia was as hot as a boiling kettle. I could not let her die like Papa and Carlo. Miss Addams is having a doctor look at her."

Her mother stared at her. "A real doctor? And how do expect to pay him?"

"We do not have to pay. He volunteers at Hull House. His name is Dr. Reynolds,

"Of course we will go back!" Her mother reached for her coat. "You do not think I will leave my child there overnight, now do you?"

and he takes care of people like us. We are to go back there and have supper and see Sophia. Please?"

At the mention of supper, Rosa perked up. "What do they eat?"

"I had soup and bread for lunch. With real butter and a big glass of milk." Luisa turned to her mother. "Can we, Mama? Can we go back?"

"Of course we will go back!" Her mother reached for her coat. "You do not think I will leave my child there overnight, do you?" She glared at Luisa, but it was a softer look than before.

Luisa hid a smile. Her mother was agreeing with her, only she did not want to show it.

When they got to Hull House, Miss Addams greeted them at the door. "Mrs. Russo, I am so happy that you have come."

Maria took Miss Addams's outstretched hand. "I understand that you have my *bambino* here."

"And a lovely *bambino* she is. Come." Miss Addams led them down the hall to the nursery at the back of the house.

And there, sitting up in her crib, was Sophia. When she saw them, she gurgled with delight. Sophia's hair still clung in damp tendrils to her forehead and cheeks, but when Luisa bent over to kiss her, her skin was cooler to the touch.

"How did you bring down her fever?" asked Luisa.

"Dr. Reynolds gave her aspirin."

"Aspirin?" The Russos looked at her in confusion. "What is aspirin?"

"It is a new drug that only came out last year. It brings down fever and cures aches and pains. Dr. Reynolds said that it was discovered by a German scientist, and that it's a miracle drug. See?" Miss Addams held out several white pills.

"How do you give a pill to a baby?" asked Rosa.

"You dissolve it in water," smiled Miss Addams. "We will give her one pill every four hours, and by morning her fever should be gone." She looked at Mrs. Russo. "May we keep her here overnight?"

Mrs. Russo looked around the room—so clean and neat. Gas lamps cast a cheery glow while a radiator under the window hissed warming steam into the air.

"Yes, that would be good." She turned to Luisa. "You will come get her tomorrow?"

Luisa nodded.

"Splendid," said Miss Addams. "Now, please come to our coffee house for some supper. And then I will ask one of our residents to give you a tour. We have many things to offer at Hull House. Now that you have found us, I hope all of you will be frequent visitors." She turned to Mrs. Russo. "Your daughter Luisa told me that she would like to go back to school."

"If you had a safe place to leave Sophia, would you allow Luisa to finish her schooling?"

"That is impossible." Mrs. Russo blinked back tears. "It is Luisa's job to look after Sophia so that Rosa and I can work."

"If you had a safe place to leave Sophia, would you allow Luisa to finish her schooling? We have a day-care program. Sophia can stay with us and be cared for while Luisa is in school."

"Mama? Could I?" Luisa grasped her mother's hand.

Mrs. Russo studied Miss Addams. *She seems to be a good and sincere woman. And Luisa is smart. With schooling, she will have a chance for a better life. She deserves that.* She turned to Miss Addams. "We can try it. Thank you."

"We have programs for you, too, and for Rosa. This is a good place to meet other women and to make friends. Come." Miss Addams took Mrs. Russo's hand and led her down the hallway.

Luisa and Rosa followed the two women. Suddenly Rosa stopped and turned on her sister. "How did you have the nerve to do this?" she whispered. "I would have never dared."

"I wanted to save Sophia."

"You are brave," Rosa said. "Maybe I can take sewing lessons here and learn to be a seamstress instead of working in the factory."

Luisa squeezed her sister's hand. They followed their mother and Miss Addams into the coffee house. It was a large wood-paneled room crammed with long tables where people sat eating, drinking coffee, and socializing.

"Please, sit." Miss Addams indicated a table where two men and three women were already seated. A large woman in a floral dress sitting across from them smiled. "Hello, I am Bella," she said in heavily accented English. "This is my husband, Thomas." She pointed to a balding man in a brown suit to her right.

"I am Maria Russo. These are my daughters Luisa and Rosa."

"Is this your first time here?" Bella leaned across the table.

"Maria, is that the sound of Italy I hear in your voice?" interrupted a man at the far end of the table.

"Si. We are from Napoli."

"Ah, Napoli!" The man kissed his fingers.

"You have been there?"

"Once." He beamed. "I was born in Pisa, and I have family in Napoli. So very beautiful…"

Luisa and Rosa exchanged delighted looks.

"Mama is making friends," said Rosa.

"Yes. Maybe she will find a husband." Luisa smiled.

"Luisa, you are scandalous!" Rosa said, laughing. Then she turned to speak to the woman on her right.

Luisa leaned back in her chair and watched her mother and sister talking and laughing. Suddenly her mother grasped her hand. "You did the right thing by disobeying me this time, Luisa. *But you should not make habit of it.*" She patted Luisa's knee and then turned back to her conversation.

Luisa smiled. Her disobedience had come from thinking for herself. *I must be growing up. And if this is growing up, I like the way it feels.* ✪

A NEW HOPE
Hull House

Jane Addams continued to work with children and for charities her whole life.

Hull House was founded in 1889 by Jane Addams and Ellen Gates Starr to help the immigrants living in Chicago's Near West Side. Jane wanted Hull House to be about neighbors helping neighbors. She believed in the dignity of all people, and in giving everyone access to opportunity. Hull House provided day care for working mothers. There were kindergarten classes in the morning, club meetings for older children in the afternoon, a public playground, classes for adults at night, and a coffee house where adults could meet and socialize.

Hull House also put on plays and art exhibits for immigrants who could not afford to attend these events on their own. By 1907, the original mansion had expanded to a thirteen-building complex that included a gymnasium, theater, music school, boys' club, auditorium, cafeteria, meeting rooms, library, kitchen, dining room, and apartments for the staff who lived there.

Jane Addams

Hull House

Chicago, Illinois

Political Activism

Jane Addams grew up in a wealthy Quaker family that believed in social justice. She graduated from Rockford University, where she received a liberal social education. On a trip to Europe she visited Toynbee Hall, a settlement house in England, and decided to dedicate her life to social causes. She attracted other similar-minded women to her cause—they worked in Hull House and were called residents. Once Hull House was established, Jane became involved in public affairs. At that time, many poor children worked in factories where conditions were unsafe. Jane and her associates fought for laws to protect children. Jane also fought for a wide range of social issues, including civil rights, women's suffrage (the right to vote), juvenile justice, and change to the justice system. She founded the Women's International League for Peace and Freedom. In 1931, Jane received the Nobel Peace Prize for her work for international peace.

A PLACE IN HISTORY

A HOUSE FOR ALL

Hull House was the first settlement house in the United States. It started a movement that grew to nearly 500 settlement houses by 1920. Hull House residents fought for laws to protect women and children. They worked to change all levels of government laws— local, state, and federal. In Chicago, they helped establish the first children's court in the United States. They fought to build neighborhood parks and branch libraries. For the state of Illinois, they worked for laws to protect women, children, and immigrants, and for compulsory education for all. Along with other settlement house leaders, they worked at the federal level to create national child labor laws, a children's bureau, and other reforms.

Credits

Care has been taken to trace ownership of copyright material contained in this book. Information enabling the publisher to rectify any reference or credit line in future editions will be welcomed.

PHOTOS AND ARCHIVAL ARTWORK: Ushistoryimages.com: 14, 24; Library of Congress: 15 (both), 25 (both), 35; Courtesy of Perkins School for the Blind, Watertown, MA: 34; historichwy49.com: 44, 45; Courtesy Son of the South: 54; Hulton Archive/Getty Images: 55; Berea College Public Relations: 64, 65; Courtesy Central Pacific Railroad Photographic History Museum, © 2011, CPRR.org: 74, 75: Johnstown Area Heritage Association/ Johnstown Flood Museum www.jaha.org: 84, 85; Jane Addams Hull-House Photographic Collection, [JAMC 0030_0855, 0007_0029, 0020_1307], University of Illinois at Chicago Library, Special Collections: 94, 95.

All other photos royalty-free (iStockphoto, Dreamstime)

COVER AND PANEL ILLUSTRATIONS: Ben Shannon

ACKNOWLEDGMENTS: Many thanks to the highly valued experts who acted as historical consultants on these stories:
Tammy Benson, Golden Spike National Historic Site; Inez Brooks-Myers, Curator, Oakland Museum of California; Richard Burkert, President, Johnstown Area Heritage Association; Lynn Downey, Historian, Levi Strauss & Co.; Graham T. Dozier, Managing Editor of Publications, Virginia Historical Society; Lisa Junkin, Education Coordinator, Jane Addams Hull-House Museum, University of Illinois at Chicago; Mary Ellyn Kunz, Museum Educator/Acting Site Administrator, Pennsbury Society; Jan Seymour-Ford, Research Librarian, Perkins School for the Blind; Kandice Watson, Co-Chair, Education & Culture Outreach Director, Oneida Indian Nation; Shannon H. Wilson, Head, Special Collections & Archives, Hutchins Library/Berea College.

Thank you to my editor, John Crossingham, and to Mary Beth Leatherdale for their invaluable insights and support.